SOPATHS

PIERS ANTHONY

Fantastic Planet Press
Portland, Oregon

Fantastic Planet Press
An Imprint of Eraserhead Press

Fantastic Planet Press
c/o Eraserhead Planet
205 NE Bryant Street
Portland, OR 97211

WWW.ERASERHEADPRESS.COM

WWW.BIZARROCENTRAL.COM

ISBN: 978-1-936383-88-7

THE SOPATHS

ALSO BY PIERS ANTHONY

FOREWORD

There has been a good deal of controversy about the so-called Fungo revolution and its founder, Abner Slate. He was accused of murdering children and fostering a sinful society. But it must also be recognized that he saved the world from the dread menace of the sopaths. Was he a hero or a criminal? Much has been written about him and the inconclusive legal cases against him, but little about his personal life, because he did his best to keep it private and out of the news. His immediate family supported him completely, and so did what became a huge personal global following that treated him almost as a religious figure. He could have become fabulously wealthy had he chosen such a course, but his integrity prevented that.

This is the inside story of that private life, based on personal interviews with Mr. Slate and those closest to him, as well as the records of Pariah, the secretive society he worked with. This will perhaps clarify some of the more alarming suspicions. Abner Slate was very much a person of his time, and it was an awful time. He did what needed to be done when it was necessary. Perhaps no more than that needs to be said of his place in history.

CHAPTER 1

Abner paused to survey the site: it was a nice suburban house surrounded by a park-like landscape. The sign said GRANVILLE VILLAGE NURSERY SCHOOL – "IT TAKES A VILLAGE." The clamor of happy children could be heard from inside.

He knocked on the door. A middle aged woman opened it. "Mr. Slate?" she inquired.

"Yes. I just wanted to inquire–"

"Of course. I am Mrs. Johnson. Please do come in."

He followed her into a small private office and took the indicated chair. "If you don't have room for another child–"

"I regret to say it isn't that, Mr. Slate. I believe in candor, and there is something I think you should know, though my colleagues advise against this." She paused significantly.

"Something about Olive," he said. He knew he was not going to like this. "I realize she is a headstrong child. That's why we felt that the experience of a good, disciplined nursery school would be appropriate."

"Ordinarily, yes. But Mr. Slate, this–this may be something else. Of course we can't be certain, nobody can be absolutely certain in a case like this, but there is strong suspicion. We simply can't afford to take the chance."

Abner tried to make his stomach muscles relax. "Take what chance?"

"The chance of the disruption her presence could cause. The–the danger."

"*What* danger?"

She visibly steeled herself. "Mr. Slate, we suspect she might be a sopath."

This caught him by surprise. "A what?"

Her mouth formed a grim smile. "You are not familiar with that term, of course." She paused again.

Abner resisted the urge to point out that his question had already adequately indicated that. "Yes."

"Now understand, we could be mistaken. It really is almost impossible to be sure. Still, considering the welfare of the other children, we must err on the side of caution."

"What is a sopath?"

"And naturally it has nothing to do with the merit of the parents. It is essentially random. So I mean absolutely no offense to you."

This was definitely what he had feared: that there was something fundamentally wrong with his child. "What is a sopath?" he repeated grimly.

"Please be patient with me, Mr. Slate. This is an extremely uncomfortable matter."

He gazed at her intently.

"I need to provide some background," she said after a moment. "Mr. Slate, are you a religious man?"

"What has that to do with this?"

"We are nondenominational, of course. But there is one aspect that relates regardless. Religious folk tend to grasp it more rapidly."

He was annoyed, but bore with it. "We attend the local Protestant church every Sunday, and support it financially. Is that answer sufficient?" He was actually a doubter, stemming from his military experience. He had seen and experienced things that no God worthy of the name would have tolerated. But that was none of her business.

"Do you believe in souls?"

This caught him entirely off-guard. "Souls?"

"More specifically, in reincarnation?"

"Reincarnation! That's not Christian."

She would not be swayed. "Do you?"

"Maybe," he agreed reluctantly. "But I did not come here

to discuss theology."

"This is beyond theology, Mr. Slate. This is a drastically secular matter at this point. But it will help if you do believe in the immortality of souls."

What could she possibly be getting at? She did not seem to be proselytizing. "Assume that I do."

"The soul normally enters a baby at birth, and remains with that person throughout life, departing only when that person dies. Then it becomes available for a new baby. Souls are immortal, as human beings are not."

"If you are trying to push a religious point, Mrs. Johnson, I will make a formal protest."

"I am not, Mr. Slate."

"There is a secular point to this?"

"Very much, Mr. Slate. It seems that souls do exist, and that the number of human souls is limited to something above six billion. Perhaps that is the limit beyond which the original generic soul can no longer be divided. Unfortunately our population has recently expanded beyond that limit. Do you understand what that means?"

"How do the extra babies acquire souls, then?"

"That is precisely the question, Mr. Slate. Some babies are born without souls, because the souls have run out. Only a minority, at present, because the deaths of souled people constantly return souls to circulation, as it were. But the number of vacancies is increasing, as the population continues to grow. The–the ratio is changing. Perhaps five years ago only one baby in ten thousand lacked a soul; now we suspect it is more like one in a hundred."

Abner dreaded her point. "And you think Olive is one of these soulless ones?"

"This is what we fear, Mr. Slate. We call them sopaths. That is a contraction of sociopaths—children without conscience. Because you see, we now know that the soul is the source of conscience."

"But isn't conscience learned?"

"Yes. But the *capacity* for it must exist. A sopath lacks that capacity. A sopath will never develop a conscience. Will never feel remorse. Never love selflessly. The only thing that moves a sopath is the prospect of immediate personal gain, and the only thing that daunts a sopath child is the threat of immediate pain or death. They are literally ungovernable, short of ugly measures. Now can you appreciate why we don't want to take your little girl?"

"Damn!" It made too much sense. He had hoped that Olive was merely wild, but she did fit the pattern this woman was describing.

"Of course we're not certain, Mr. Slate. I hope we are mistaken. But we feel we must not take the risk. Do you understand?"

"Yes," he said tightly. "How did you identify her, after only a brief interview?"

"We have had experience. One sopath is more than enough to alert a person. But I repeat, we are not sure of your child. All children are selfish; it takes time to distinguish natural childishness from incorrigibility. But it's a calculated risk that we feel we can't afford."

The woman was after all being practical. "I fear you are right. Assuming Olive is a–a sopath–what can we do about it? How should we handle the situation?"

"Mr. Slate, it is not my place to advise you on such a thing."

"What should we do?" he repeated firmly.

"I can give only an opinion, which may be erroneous or inapplicable to your case."

He was tired of evasions. "What?"

"Mr. Slate, there is only one treatment we know, and only one cure. The treatment is permanent incarceration, in the manner of a rabid animal. You must cage her."

"We can't do that. What's the cure?"

The woman winced as she spoke. "Death."

"You're telling us to kill our baby."

Mrs. Johnson backed off immediately. "I shouldn't have

said that. I apologize."

He shook his head. "You said what you meant."

"I didn't want to say it. Surely I am wrong. How can anyone destroy a little child?"

How, indeed! Yet he had done it while serving overseas. He had been a sergeant, trying to protect his complement from surprise attack. They had pursued a suspected young sniper, who had fled into a house and not emerged. They had a mission to accomplish, and could not afford to be ambushed on their return. They had to take out the sniper, and could not take time to lay siege to the premises. "Burn the house," he had ordered tersely. They had done so, then discovered it was an orphanage. Several children were burned to death. The suspected sniper was merely an older child spying on the foreign troops. The horror of it had haunted him for months.

Abner stood. "Thank you for your candor, Mrs. Johnson. I think we do have a problem."

She stood too. "I fear I said too much. It is not my business to diagnose any such condition."

He saw what was bothering her. "I will consider this interview to be private. I thank you for your information, uncomfortable as it is."

"And of course I'm not recommending that you—"

She could get in trouble with the law for suggesting that a child be killed. "Of course. I will seek other information."

She nodded. "That would be appreciated."

Abner drove home, deep in thought. He hated the notion, but knew that the woman had spoken truth. Olive was incorrigible. He had not wanted to believe it, but too much was falling into place. The nursery school woman had not offered a revelation so much as confirmation. Now he had a name for it: sopath. One who was sociopathic. Not crazy, merely without conscience. There were others like her. And a rationale: she lacked a soul. It was not the fault of her upbringing, but of the accident of timing. She had arrived when no soul was available, missing her window of opportunity. Apparently souls did not offer twice. Maybe it occurred at the moment of birth, and thereafter the avenue into the baby was closed off. A practical rather than a religious thing.

Zelda met him at the door, wearing a bathrobe. She looked the question. He shook his head.

"Damn!" she said, echoing his own reaction. "I know it seems unloving, but I wanted to have her out of the house for a few hours at a time, so I could relax."

"Where is she now?"

"Asleep. She does get tired after rampaging, fortunately. It's a small blessing."

"Jasper?"

"Playing a video. He'll be entranced for at least an hour."

"You knew we'd have to talk."

She nodded. "It has been too pervasive, too rough. I feared what you would learn."

"With justice. Have you heard the word 'sopath' before?"

"Yes," she said grimly. "That's what I feared. I overheard two women talking at the store. Incorrigible?"

"If she is one. They're not sure."

"She is one. Is there any treatment?"

"They—they said she had to be caged—or killed. That once a sopath is born, there's no further chance for a soul, and therefore there can be no conscience. It will just get worse."

Her eyes were fixed. "Abner, before we—we continue this discussion—can we take a break?"

"A break?"

She let her robe fall open, showing her bare breasts.

Surprised, Abner did a quick assessment. Zelda, unlike most women, grew passionate when stressed. It was her way of diverting the bad feeling. This was bad news, but he could not demur.

In moments they were at it, making desperate love. Zelda was a well-formed woman, always a pleasure to see and touch. But he wished there could have been some other occasion for this delight.

As they concluded, there was a sound. Both of them paused, but it seemed to be nothing, so they relaxed.

"You were saying?" she inquired as she cleaned up. Her mood had definitely improved.

"They have had experience. They won't take a sopath. The term is a contraction of sociopath, and it means a hopeless case. They say it's not our fault; she just happened to be born when there wasn't a soul available."

"Caged or killed," she repeated as she dressed. "Abner, I can't do either of those things. She's our child."

"I know." He spread his hands. "We'll just have to watch her. Closely."

"But how can I get a job if I can't leave her alone?"

"Maybe there's a facility for them. A place where they know how to handle them."

"Like a prison?" she asked sharply.

"Like a reform school."

"She's only three years old!"

And that was only part of the problem. "We'll think of something," he said with obviously false hope.

She opened the door, stepped into the hall, and screamed.

Abner leaped to join her. There was blood spreading from Jasper's room. "I'll handle it," he said, steering her back into the bedroom. She went without protest.

He looked into Jasper's room. The boy was sprawled across his bed, bathed in blood. A pool of it was jelling on the floor, extending to the doorway. The boy's throat had been slit.

Abner leaped to the small figure. The blood was still spilling out. He caught a fold of the sheet in his hand and clapped it to Jasper's throat. He felt a faint pulse. Had he stopped it in time?

"Zelda!" he called. "Call an ambulance! He's alive but fading." Then he held on, holding the boy's remaining blood inside while waiting.

Zelda got on the phone, and soon the ambulance arrived. Abner got out of the way and let Zelda handle it. She was competent, now that there was something positive to do. If the boy had been dead, it would have been another matter.

Numb, Abner walked to Olive's room. She was just finishing a candy bar. There was a spot of blood on her nightie.

He kept his voice level. "Where did you get that bar, Olive?"

"From Jasper," she answered matter-of-factly, licking her fingers.

"Did he give it to you?"

"No."

"How did you get it from him?"

"I snucked behind him and cut his throat and took it."

"Olive, you shouldn't do that."

She continued licking her fingers, ignoring him. And of course it was a stupid thing to say. The word "should" had no meaning for her, only "can." Jasper had had something she wanted, and wouldn't give it to her, so she had taken it. By almost killing him.

He closed the door and walked back to the bedroom. Zelda was standing where he had left her, facing away as the medic continued to stabilize the boy. "That sound," she said.

What could he tell her? "Maybe you better lie down. I'll call the police."

"They have already done that. I'll go to the hospital with Jasper. I just want to know."

There was no way out. "She tried to kill him."

She nodded. "Why?"

"She wanted his candy bar."

She shuddered. "Tell them it was an accident."

Because even after this she couldn't stand to do what they had to do. He knew better, but couldn't have her freaking out right now. "Okay."

They took Jasper away, and Zelda went with them.

Abner waited. If they had gotten over there when they heard the sound, would they have been in time? He suspected not. The child had "snucked" up behind her older brother with the knife while he was preoccupied with the video game, and sliced his throat. Had she even asked for the candy bar? Probably not, as she knew he wouldn't share. The sound might have been him collapsing on the bed, or her departing the room with the candy bar.

They should have locked her in her room until they could watch her. They had been caught short by that lapse.

The police surveyed the scene. They found the knife where it lay under a sheet. It would have Olive's fingerprints on it. "They were playing," Abner said. "We didn't realize the knife was real. It was a horrible accident."

The man nodded. He spoke into his radio. "Sopath. Come clean it up."

So they knew about sopaths. How was it that the news had never become public? But Abner knew the answer: to avoid panic. They were keeping it quiet, because the problem had no ready solution.

The man turned to Abner. "Keep it locked up." He departed.

"It," not "her." Yet who could say they were wrong? Abner went and locked Olive's door.

It took hours for the numbness to wear off, gradually replaced by pain. They had almost lost their son, murdered by their daughter. What were they to do?

Zelda returned from the hospital. "He's in intensive care, scheduled for surgery. I couldn't watch or do anything. But I had to do something, so I came home. Olive needs care."

"You know we can't just ignore what happened. The police said—"

"I know what they said. But I can't do it. We'll just have to make it safe."

Safe for whom? But he let it pass.

They carried on as if nothing had happened. The police cleanup crew had restored the crime scene to pristine quality. There was no further evidence of the disaster. Except for the absence of Jasper.

Zelda fixed a meal for Olive. Neither adult was in a mood to eat, but the child gobbled down her food with gusto. It was clear that she felt no remorse for her dreadful act.

But when it was time for her bath, she said no. Zelda didn't try to reason or argue with her. "If you don't get in the tub, I will put you in."

"I'll bite."

"Then I'll hold your face under the water."

The child gazed at her mother appraisingly. Zelda's eyes were focused on distance and her mouth was a thin line. Olive decided to take her bath.

So had it been a bluff? Abner wasn't sure. Zelda was like a zombie at the moment, but the wrong nudge could send her into an ugly fit. Olive had realized that, and taken the expedient course. To her mind, drowning was a feasible mechanism, if one had the power to enforce it. Zelda was normally a gentle person, but she had been pushed to her limit. Much as Abner had been when going after a fleeing figure who might have gunned down one of his men. It did not require many such ambushes to evoke deadly toughness in the objects of such mischief.

When the child was done, Zelda returned to the hospital. "I have to be sure of Jasper," she explained tightly, kissing him on the way out. "I have locked her in. Don't let her out."

"Understood."

As soon as the car departed, Olive called. "Daaady!"

"Go to sleep," he called back.

"I want out!"

"Mother's orders."

"I don't care!"

"Just settle down. She'll return later tonight."

"No!"

She was in a temper, but that was standard for her. He tried to tune out her continued calls, and went to watch the TV. But it didn't work; she was persistent and loud. She banged on the door, screaming.

He couldn't stop himself from listening. Olive alternated tearful appeals with shouted threats. She was only three years old, but already had a small arsenal of persuasions. And no conscience. What were they going to do with her?

At last she tired and went silent, but Abner's thoughts did not ease. They couldn't keep her locked up all the time. There had to be a more permanent solution. The one he didn't want to face. Mrs. Johnson had said it, before trying to back off: Death.

Was he to kill his own child, as he had those orphans? The orphans had been inadvertent; this would be deliberate.

No. There had to be some viable alternative.

Zelda returned home in two hours. "It doesn't look good," she reported grimly. "He's in a coma. They say he lost too much blood. There may have been--"

"Brain damage?"

She nodded. "There's nothing we can do but wait. And hope." She paused, then seemed to force herself to ask what she had to. "Olive?"

"Locked in. She screamed herself into exhaustion."

"I had better check on her."

"Maybe you should let her be, since she's quiet now."

"That's the best time to check her."

He had to agree. She went to Olive's room and unlocked the door. She was back in a moment. "Sleeping like a little angel."

"She's a little demon."

Then she was crying. He tried to comfort her, but in this respect she was like her daughter: she fussed herself to sleep.

He didn't want to disturb her, so he continued holding her, lying on the bed in their clothing. Whatever they faced, they had to have their rest.

But as he faded into sleep himself, he wondered: had she locked the door again after checking on Olive? He wanted to check, but would have had to disturb Zelda to do so. That was too much of a sacrifice.

The phone rang in the wee hours. Zelda leaped up to answer it before Abner really had time to orient himself. She listened for a moment, then set it down, her face drawn. "He's dead."

It took him a moment to orient. Then he was stunned. "Jasper!"

There was a commotion downstairs: a crash and a scream. Zelda, already on her feet, lurched out the door and into the darkness of the hall.

Abner had a horrible premonition. Some children really *were* assassins. Sopaths could be. "I'll go!" he cried. But she continued toward the stairs.

He rolled to his feet and followed. He heard Zelda cry out. Then he heard her tumbling down the stairs. He turned on the hall light, which she had ignored in her haste, but of course that was too late.

Zelda was at the foot of the stairs, lying askew. As if it were a snapshot he saw her there—and saw the cord that had been tied across the top step from the banister support to the rail on the wall. She had tripped over it in the shadow and fallen headlong.

He ripped out the cord and charged down to help her. But already he knew with a sickened certainty that it was useless. Her head was at a wrong angle and she wasn't breathing.

And there stood Olive, gazing placidly on the scene. She had of course tied the cord for exactly this purpose: to injure or kill an adult.

"Get up into your room," he snapped at the child.

"No."

He rose and grabbed her with one motion. For an instant he was tempted to hurl her into a wall, but he simply carried her up the stairs and dropped her on the bed. He locked the door.

He called the police. The same crew came to investigate. "I told you to keep it locked up," the man reproved him.

"My wife forgot." It was like being in an unreal realm.

"Don't *you* forget."

When they and Zelda's body were gone, Abner tried to relax, to fathom the magnitude of the disaster, but it eluded him. He found himself half-believing that none of it had happened, that Zelda and Jasper were out shopping for school clothes and would return shortly. That gave him a temporary license on sanity.

Then Olive pounded on her door. "Let me out, daddy! I'll be good."

And how was he to deal with this little monster? She had killed twice, without remorse. Yet she was his daughter.

He went to her bedroom and unlocked the door. She was standing there, unconscionably cute. "Why did you tie that rope?" he asked as she walked out.

"She locked me in."

"So did I."

Her little head turned to gaze at him with disquieting consideration. "I don't like it. I'm hungry." She made her way down the stairs, navigating them carefully, as they were quite big for her.

So it had indeed been deliberate. Olive knew the stairs were dangerous, so had cleverly used them to get back at her mother. He would have thought that such strategy would be beyond a three-year-old, but evidently it was not. And so a little child had been able to kill another child and an adult, because they had annoyed her.

He followed her down to the kitchen. He went for cereal and milk. He was not great on making meals, but could handle this much.

"No," she said firmly. "Candy."

"Candy isn't good for you."

"I don't care."

So he fetched her a candy bar. Was she to govern this household, having eliminated those who told her no? Would she become a little tyrant whose whim was law?

There was no point in dragging this out. "Now use the

bathroom if you need to, and return to your room."

"No."

He gave her a direct stare. "Or else."

"Or else what?"

Was she calling his bluff? "Or else I'll spank you so hard you won't ever forget it."

She considered, then obeyed. She understood ruthless power. Unfortunately that seemed to be all she responded to.

That reminded him again of his military service. He had turned out to be a natural leader, with a special touch for female personnel, and gotten promoted rapidly as others died from sniping and roadside bombs. They had been under siege by urban guerrillas, never knowing when the next enemy strike would come. That had worn down the men and women. They had a higher attrition from post traumatic stress and suicide than from enemy action. Abner had to his own surprise been able to handle it, armor-plating his spirit after the sniping episode. But he hated it, and was heartily glad when his term expired and he returned to civilian life. About the only thing he had missed was the women. He had been careful never to abuse his authority, but they had come to him, some of them beautiful, including even a few who ranked him, and there had been many warm nights. It was a case of eat, drink, and be merry, for tomorrow we die, and it seemed to affect the women as much as the men.

Now he was under siege again, by his own vicious child. His old toughness of mind was returning. He still hated it, but knew he could do what he had to.

Once Olive was locked in, he got on the phone. Half an hour satisfied him that there was no institution ready to take a child without conscience. The word about sopaths was already getting around.

But he had a job to go to, and he couldn't leave her home all day. Neither locked up nor loose. He had to settle this soon. Just as he had had to when on the mission. He had already experienced the consequences of not acting with sufficient force. Twice.

He couldn't just kill her, or leave her to die. Yet something had to be done. There was no other way.

He phoned work. "Something has come up. I can't make it in today."

"We heard," his boss said. "Horrible accident. Your wife."

"Yes. There are things to handle."

"We understand. Come back when you can."

How nice to have an understanding employer! But that tolerance was limited. He would have to report for work in a few days, or lose his job. That meant he had to deal with the sopath soon.

He pondered, and concluded that he needed to give Olive early reason to kill him. When he caught her in the act, he would be able to do what had to be done. To burn out the sniper.

He rehearsed it in his mind. He did not like it, but saw no feasible alternative. He was at war.

He let her out at lunch. "This time you will have a nutritious meal," he announced. He had it laid out: milk, bread, salad.

"No."

"Yes. Eat it."

"No!" She swept it off the table with her arm.

He picked her up, put her over his knee, and gave her a hard spanking, exactly as he had threatened before. She screamed as much in outrage as pain. Then he carried her up and dumped her on the bed, slamming the door as he left her bedroom.

He went to the kitchen and cleaned up the mess. Then he went to his own bedroom, lay down on the bed, and closed his eyes.

It didn't take her long to get moving. He tracked her by the sounds. She checked the door, discovered that he had forgotten to lock it, and went out, trying to be quiet. The notion that he might have left it unlocked on purpose was beyond her mental capacity. She was a vicious animal, but also a child.

She went downstairs, where the kitchen knives remained

within reach of a stool. He hadn't thought of the knives, but would have left them there if he had. She came quietly upstairs.

She peeked into his room. He watched her through slitted eyes, faking sleep. She came quietly close, lifting the knife. She was going for the throat; it had worked before, so was a proven technique. She held the knife with both little hands and brought it down in a slicing motion.

He caught her arms. She screamed with surprise and fell back. He caught her by the ankles, picked her up, and swung her in a half circle, cracking her head into the chest of drawers. He dropped her, suddenly feeling acute remorse. How could he be doing this?

But it was too late. Her neck was broken, and she was dead.

He picked up the phone, calling the police again. "This is Abner Slate. I have just murdered my daughter. Come and get me."

"On our way." There was no special surprise in the voice.

They came a third time. "Dead, all right," the man said.

"I am ready to go."

"You bashed her?"

"Yes."

The man faced him. "Mr. Slate, what happened here was an accident. You have suffered a terrible triple loss. We'll clean it up and write up the report. You just take it easy and keep your mouth shut."

"But you have to arrest me!"

"For doing what you had to do? It was an accident."

"But I killed her! I bashed her head! I murdered my child!" But the worst of it was that he had planned that killing, knowing there was no real choice.

The man put a firm hand on his shoulder. "Settle down, Mr. Slate. You destroyed a sopath. That's not murder. It's a public service. You've got grief enough with the loss of your wife and son without our complicating it. Set your affairs in order and get on with your life. There will be no report unless you force our hand. We don't want a disturbance, so don't bruit it about. That's all."

Stunned anew, Abner sat down. "Just like that? No investigation? No report?"

"We know the signs," the man said. "That girl was one. If you had killed her first, your family would still be alive. But we knew you wouldn't believe until you had experience. That's the way it is. Remember that, next time you see a sopath."

Abner could appreciate that. "I'll try to warn the family the sopath is in. But they won't believe until it's too late."

The man nodded, experienced in this. "But you can notify us. That may help. We try to track them."

The police departed after their crew removed the body. Abner sat for a long time, trying to come to grips with it. He had indeed killed a child again, this time deliberately. This time his own little daughter. The police had evidently forgiven him, but how could he forgive himself?

Yet the policeman had been correct: if he had nerved himself to do it sooner, he would not now be numb with grief for his wife and son. Could he forgive himself for that, either?

CHAPTER 2

The rest of the day passed in a daze of grief, remorse, confusion, and bleak nothingness. Abner must have eaten, then slept. What else was there to do? His world had been destroyed in a single day. He knew he was in shock, but functioning. Though he wasn't sure how long that would continue.

He tried to call members of his wider family, to let them know what had happened and perhaps garner some moral support. But he was unable to get through to any of them. He knew why: somehow they had already gotten the word, and put a block on his number. They did not want to talk to him. They regarded him as a murderer who had gotten away with it. Or they knew about the sopath, and wanted no part of it.

Actually, he understood. He suspected that he would have reacted similarly had one of them brutally killed their own child. He would not have been open to an explanation about a total lack of conscience. How could a little child be judged that way? He might not have openly condemned them, because family was family, but he would have avoided them, yes, like the plague.

He was on his own.

The night was interminable, alone on the double bed. He dreamed of Zelda, knowing she was dead. He relived his awful murder of Olive. Only three years old, yet a merciless killer. Had he but known...

Yet he had known, or should have known. Olive had been a little bitch from the time she had opportunity. At first they had dismissed it as the natural selfishness of a baby. In retrospect he saw that they had been in denial about her real nature.

They hadn't wanted to see her as she was, a creature without a conscience or the capacity to develop one. A child whose initial utter selfishness would never be ameliorated by time or nurturing.

They had paid for that denial with the wipeout of the family.

In the morning Abner had come to a decision: he would never again be in denial about anything. He would exert rational control and see all things as clearly as he possibly could. Had he done that before, he could have saved his family. Now, belatedly, he would do it, in honor of that lost family. Otherwise their dreadful passing would be for nothing.

He got up, shaved, dressed, had some breakfast, and moved through the normal morning routine, unable to focus on any larger objective. He was on automatic pilot, and that was fine. It allowed him to function, for the time being.

The phone rang.

He picked it up. "Hello." He sounded normal to his own ear, to his surprise.

"Mr. Slate? I am Sylvia, of Pariah."

A damned solicitation for a charity! He was in no mood. "Sorry, no." He started to hang up.

"Please, Mr. Slate. I really need to talk to you. I'll be there in fifteen minutes."

"But—" But now she had hung up.

He sighed. It wasn't as if he had anything else to do. He would listen to her spiel, gently tell her no, and be rid of her. He had problems of his own.

The doorbell rang in exactly fifteen minutes. He answered, dully. There was one small silver lining: here was a person who didn't know, so it was a regular interaction, providing the illusion of normalcy.

She was a woman of about his own age, thirty, smartly garbed, undistinguished. She didn't wait on him. "Mr. Slate, I must talk to you about sopaths."

So much for normalcy. She knew. "Come in," he said numbly.

She took a seat in the living room and started talking without social preamble. "You have lost your family. The only reason you survive is because you killed the sopath. Others, even your own relatives, don't understand. You have become a social outcast. You are in shock. You don't know what you'll do tomorrow, let alone the future. You need help."

Obviously someone had told her. "You have help?" he asked somewhat dryly.

"I do, Mr. Slate. I represent Pariah. This is an organization of survivors of sopath infestation. We are all pariahs. We help each other in any and all ways necessary, to enable us to survive and eventually prosper."

Suddenly he was interested. "You suffered—similarly?"

"Let me clarify that at Pariah we have a policy of Don't Ask. That is, don't ask the details of a particular person's experience with the sopath. They are universally ugly. But we can tell our own cases, if we choose, and receive a sympathetic and empathetic hearing. So I will tell you mine. It was last year. I had three children, and the youngest was a boy I thought was just being difficult, as they can be at that age. The terrible twos, you know. Then he started killing his older siblings. When he put rat poison in my husband's drink—" She shook herself. "My eyes were finally opened. I did what I had to do, though it was the hardest thing I ever had to do in my life. I filled the bathtub and held the devil child under until he drowned. Then I vomited, cleaned up, and turned myself in."

"And the police brushed you off," Abner said.

"Exactly. My family cut me off. The police have known about the sopath menace for some time, but kept a lid on it so that the public won't panic. I think this policy is a disaster, as it guarantees that families will continue to suffer as mine did." She looked at him. "As yours did."

"You do understand," he agreed.

He wasn't sure exactly how it happened, but then he was in her arms, sobbing while she comforted him. There was nothing romantic or sexual about it, and they weren't even friends. It was simply a necessary release.

"We all have to let go sometime," she said as they separated. "The multiple horrors overwhelm us."

"Thank you," he said as he wiped his face. It was a small blessing in the inferno of hell to have an understanding person. "You were saying?"

She picked up as if there had been no interruption. "So I formed a local chapter of Pariah, which is a quiet global organization without official status or many paid personnel, doing what needs to be done on a voluntary basis. Social organizations and the police inform us of new cases, and we step in. We seek no publicity. We have no pride; we merely do what is necessary. It does seem to give our ruined lives meaning. We will help you if you want it, and expect you to contribute what you can. The need is constant and growing, unfortunately."

"You are a kind of family," Abner said.

"We are," she agreed. "We are widely diverse, with a few things in common apart from the dreadful one. We are of reproductive age, we are suffering, and we understand. That last is what binds us together." She gave him a straight look. "Mr. Slate, no one at Pariah will condemn you or avoid you. We all have similar sorrow, shame, or criminality, whatever one chooses to call it. All you have to do is join. There is no formal membership, but we do have meetings on a daily basis, just pariahs getting together, helping with new cases. I will give you my address so that you can come in when you are ready. There is no obligation."

"I'm ready now," Abner said with sudden decision. This was exactly what he needed.

She hesitated. "I would take you in now to show you our literature and facilities, and have you meet other members, but I have another call to make. It is the nature of these things that they should not wait long. The—the suicide rate is high. I would have come for you yesterday, but there were children to pick up. We are especially sensitive about newly orphaned children."

"I understand. I'll come with you."

She nodded. "As you wish. My car is outside. You can follow in yours."

He did. She led him to another section of town. There was the smoking ruin of a house that had just burned down. The sooty hulk of the car showed where the garage had been. The fire truck was just departing.

Sylvia parked, and Abner parked behind her. They went to the house. There was a woman on her knees beside the ashes, her face in her hands, sobbing uncontrollably. No one was comforting her. No neighbors had gathered. That gave Abner the hint already: there had been a sopath in the house.

"Mrs. Falcon," Sylvia said.

The wretched woman didn't seem to hear her, unsurprisingly.

"Bunty Falcon," Sylvia repeated more loudly. "I am Sylvia. I represent Pariah."

The woman noticed her. She tried to get to her feet, but fell on the ground, too distraught to make it alone. Her hair and bathrobe were coated with ashes, her face streaked with grime and tears. Abner felt guilty for noticing the flash of her well-formed legs as the robe parted.

"I'll help." Abner stepped in and put his hands on the woman's shoulders, carefully heaving her to her feet. It was in part his way of masking his embarrassment for his peek, though he hoped it had gone unnoticed. How could he be tuning in on legs, in the throes of his own grief?

She had caught her balance; he could tell by the shifting of her stance. He tried to let her go, but she turned into him, flung her arms around his body, and sobbed into his shoulder. Pretty much as he had done with Sylvia.

He stood there, holding her, his awareness of her slender torso compounding his guilt. She needed honest comfort, not masculine appreciation. He looked over her shoulder at Sylvia.

Sylvia nodded. "Let it be," she murmured. "Whatever is needed."

He had become a member of Pariah. He discovered that

this eased his own pain to a degree. He was helping another person, a woman who had evidently lost not only her family, but her home, her car, clothing, everything. She was worse off than he was.

After a time, the woman calmed and drew back a little, without stepping clear of his embrace. "I—I apologize. I am normally a very rational, self-possessed person. I was just so overwhelmed." Her face, under the dirt and dark, frazzled hair, was becoming, like a work of art amidst ruins.

"No need," he said. "I understand. I just lost my own family similarly. I am suffering too."

She essayed a faint smile. "Bunty."

"Abner. Maybe you had better come home with me. For now. Until the insurance—your home—"

She made no pretense of hesitation. She knew her situation was dire. "Thank you. I appreciate the kindness of a stranger."

He looked questioningly at Sylvia. "That is exactly how it works," she said. "Come to my house tomorrow, both of you. Here is my card." She pressed it into his hand.

Thus simply he was driving Bunty to his house. It seemed to be the proper thing to do. She was a total stranger, but he understood what she was suffering.

"Before you take me in, there's something I need to tell you," she said as she rode beside him.

"The policy is not to inquire," he said. "It's a painfully private matter."

"But I have to tell you. I murdered my son."

"I murdered my daughter. She was a sopath."

"We had heard of them, of sopaths, but were in denial. But when the house burned—he had locked the doors and windows—we never expected anything like that! It was sheer chance that I had gotten up early to use the toilet. I smelled the smoke and ran downstairs, not realizing how serious it was. I picked up a chair and bashed out a window and leaped through before the smoke got me. I ran around the house, somehow hoping my husband and daughter had escaped before me, but they hadn't. Then I saw him there, still holding the gasoline can, watching the fire and chortling."

"They have no conscience," he reminded her. "They can kill from anger when disciplined."

"I was so enraged that I came up behind him, picked him up, and heaved him headfirst through the window into the burning house. He must have been stunned by the impact, because he never even screamed. He died in the fire. Now you know. I am a murderer. If you prefer to take me to the police station--"

"They won't listen," he said. "My sopath daughter came after me with a kitchen knife. I held her by her feet and swung her head into a dresser. I must have broken her neck. She had already killed my wife and son."

"You do understand," she said, shuddering.

"Oh, yes, God help me."

"God help us both," she agreed.

They continued in silence.

At the house he showed her briefly around. "It's not fancy, and not cleaned up for visitors. It—it happened just yesterday. I haven't paid attention."

"Could I—if you don't mind—clean up a bit?"

"Of course! Use the upstairs bathroom. It's got soap and towels. You'll need clothing—you're about my wife's size. Just rummage for what you need. She won't be needing it anymore." Then, overcome by sudden grief, he turned away.

"I truly understand. Thank you."

Abner gave himself over to the emotion, knowing it was best to experience it rather than try to suppress it. Before long, wrung out, he recovered equilibrium. He sat in the living room, feeling almost like a guest in his own home, listening to the sound of the shower followed by the hair dryer and the squeak of the bedroom closet door. A third time he felt guilt for imagining her nude. He had no business thinking of her that way. Not now in his grief. Not ever.

In due course Bunty reappeared. Abner took a breath.

She was in one of Zelda's outfits, clean, with her damp hair spread out about her shoulders in a dusky cloud. She more than fit the clothing, which she must have cinched here and let out there to accommodate her figure. She was beautiful.

"All right?" she inquired gently.

Abner felt himself blushing. "Was I staring? I'm sorry."

"Don't be concerned. I have been known to have that effect on men. I didn't mean to overdo it."

"Thank you for understanding," he said weakly.

"Let me explain that I am the type of person who maintains control during an emergency, then collapses once whatever needs to be done is done. I will collapse again tonight. Fair warning."

"Warning taken," he said. "I'm the same way. I will give you whatever distance you need. Just treat my house as yours. It needs the attention of a woman."

"Now let's see what needs doing." In a moment she was exploring the kitchen, especially the cupboards and refrigerator. "You are low on supplies."

"Zelda was going to grocery shop today." He was suddenly overwhelmed again, and had to sit down. "Sorry. Right now I seem to lack your ability to stiff it out. But I recover quickly."

"Of course. We had better shop now."

"I don't really know what to get. Zelda always handled it."

"Not your department," she agreed. "But it is mine. If you will take me to the store, I'll shop. I'm afraid I will have to use your money. My purse was lost, with my money and ID. It will take time to untangle that."

Abner didn't argue. He drove her to the store, and she circulated through it with authority, knowing what she wanted. He gave her money, and she used it efficiently. They returned with a grocery bag full.

Back at his house, she fixed him a nice lunch. This made him feel awkward. "This is—you really don't need to—" he protested.

"This is something I need to do," she said.

"I appreciate it."

In the afternoon they talked. Bunty was alert and clever,

evoking similar qualities in him. He liked her. Then she lay on the couch and slept, fitfully. They had, it seemed, settled in.

He gazed at her as she slept, admiring her form. It was simply an automatic male response to a woman who looked like her. She had mentioned along the way that she was thirty, his age, and in repose the lines of her face did hint at it. But she had by no means lost the bloom of youth. Her knees were drawn up, her skirt was bunched around her rear, and it was one fine example of its kind. He shouldn't be looking.

Tomorrow they would go to Sylvia's house, other arrangements would be made, and Bunty would be out of his life. Then he would be alone again.

He dreaded the prospect. At least today he had some distraction, of whatever nature. He needed that.

She woke after an hour. "Oh, I think the afternoon is gone," she said, chagrined. "I shouldn't have slept."

"You needed it. You have had a terrible day."

"A terrible morning. You have been kind, and I truly appreciate it."

He spread his hands. "I appreciate the company. It makes the awfulness retreat."

"Yes. Let me see about dinner." She got up and went to the kitchen. He let her.

It was another nice meal. She did know her business. She even took care of the dishes, which had accumulated in the past day.

Then it was evening and time to retire. "I'll fetch a blanket and pillow for the couch," he said.

"Why?"

"So you can have the bedroom."

"We will share the bedroom."

"But it's a double bed."

"Room for both of us."

He shook his head. "I'm not sure you understand. You're a comely woman. If I share the bed with you, I will get ideas. I know we're both in severe grief, but it's a male thing. I react despite knowing better."

"Exactly."

"What?" he asked, confused.

"Abner, you are being kind to me. I mean to return the favor. We may never see each other again after tomorrow, but while we are together I will do my part. I am not a woman of many talents, but this is something I do know how to do. Please let me do it. I have seen you looking. I will not be a tease. It is not as if either of us can be unfaithful to our spouses, and we will not be, in our hearts."

He was dumbfounded. "Are you saying?"

"I am." She took his hand and led him to the bedroom.

He tried to demur. "This—this really isn't necessary. I brought you here because I saw how desperately you need-ed help, and I knew you wouldn't get it from your family or friends. I did not have sex in mind, and I think it would be wrong to ask it of you."

"Exactly," she repeated.

"I don't understand."

"You did a generous thing. You're a nice man. I have known you only hours, but that's long enough to take your measure in key respects. You're decent, and you like sex. You will never clasp your wife again, nor I my husband. It is better for us both to be realistic, and fulfill each other's needs."

"Isn't that like doing it for pay?"

She nodded. "Not for money, in this case, but for mutual advantage. It's a fair analogy."

"Not one I like."

"There is nothing about this situation that either of us likes. If we could wave a wand and restore our families, we'd do it instantly. But we can't. We are up against a new reality. The faster we adjust to it, the better off we will be. That's simply common sense."

"Common sense!"

"I'll be a weak woman before long, as I mentioned. At the moment I am riding the hard rail of necessity. This is some-thing I need to do for you."

"You *don't* need to do it!" he protested.

"My realism says I do. Please, further argument will simply make it more difficult."

He realized that she was determined. She was certainly desirable. There were limits to his decency. "If that's the way you want it."

She grimaced. "I don't *want* any part of it. But I have to do it. I don't think I can kiss you; that's too intimate. But I can do the rest."

"I still don't know—"

She disrobed so efficiently that it was as if her clothing had dissolved. She stood splendidly nude before him. "Will you undress, or do you prefer me to do it for you?"

Something clicked into place. "If you really mean to do this, then you can prove it by undressing me. You can stop at any time and I will not pursue you."

"A fair compromise," she agreed. She approached him and started removing his clothing, beginning with his shirt.

"You've done this before," he said, not really surprised.

"It was a game with my husband. He liked to be seduced." She tackled his shoes, making him lift one foot and then the other. Then she addressed his trousers.

"My wife became passionate when upset," he said. "It was her way of coping."

"I like your wife." The trousers dropped to his feet, and he stepped out of them.

She drew down his undershorts. His penis sprang out, fully erect. "The—she was on the pill."

"So am I." She stroked his member, encouraging it to further rigidity.

"Lubricant helped."

"I have applied it." She stooped to kiss the tip.

She really was prepared. "I am running out of excuses."

"I noticed." She drew him down on the bed. He found himself kissing her fine breasts, which had somehow come up against his face. Then she guided him to mount her, and her hands steered his eager member. Suddenly he was inside her, with volcanic urgency.

There followed a sequence such as he had hardly dared imagine. It seemed he would never stop pumping out fluid, encouraged by her rhythmic contractions. She was correct: she did know how to do it.

He subsided, gasping, but remained connected. She held him close against her, his head beside hers. He did not try to kiss her mouth, per her preference. He doubted she had climaxed with him; her action had been for him alone. That was about the only way the experience fell short of perfection.

They cleaned up after, and lay down on the bed again, she in Zelda's pajamas. "Are you satisfied?" she asked.

"Oh, yes," he agreed, amazed.

"Understand, this next has nothing to do with you or your performance. I am letting go."

"Letting go?"

Then she burst into tears.

Oh. She had warned him. She had accomplished her duties as she saw them, then collapsed. All he could do was lie there beside her, letting her do what she had to do.

"Please, if you would," she said. "Hold me."

He put his arms around her as well as he could as she turned into him and sobbed into his shoulder. He was conscious of her soft breasts beneath the pajamas, pressing against his chest. Yet again he felt guilty for noticing, despite the recent sex, when what she needed was comforting. So did he, actually, but holding her like this was comforting him too. He could almost pretend she was Zelda.

Soon she slept, and he did too.

In the morning he woke to find their mouths together. They were kissing!

He drew his face back. "I'm sorry. I didn't mean to do that."

"It's all right, Abner. You didn't do it. I did."

"You kissed me?"

"Last night I couldn't. This morning my subconscious

seems to have accepted you. Do you want more sex?"

He was taken aback. "I—no, thanks."

Her hand felt down to touch his member through the pajamas. "You lie. Give me a moment." She got up and went to the bathroom.

In moments she returned, nude, and surely prepared. She got down on him, found his member, brought it out from the pajamas, and slipped it into her. This time she kissed him as she brought him to climax. It had been only a few hours since the last time, but the novelty made it almost as explosive. He felt pulse after pulse of ejaculate forging into her. She wasn't Zelda, but she was more than good enough.

She remained with him until the last ebb was out, still kissing him. Then she got up again and he heard her running the shower. She was nothing if not efficient.

She fixed breakfast while he showered and dressed. She had settled in amazingly quickly. He might have felt resentful, but instead was relieved. Alone, he would have been transfixed by grief. As it was, that was only one thing amidst competing interests.

"I need to be candid," Bunty said when breakfast was done. "Yesterday morning I was wiped out. You extended a hand, gave me a place to stay the night, made me feel almost normal between bouts of self pity. I am deeply appreciative."

"You're welcome," he said. "I thought I was doing you a favor, but having you here has eased my own wipe-out. I will be sorry to see you go."

"Must I go?"

"No!" he said before thinking. "I mean, I have no right to hold on to you, but your company has done as much for me as anything I have done for you. As you said, neither of us would have chosen this path, but given that we were thrust into it, I am immensely grateful for your company."

"I had hoped you would feel that way. But I have to be honest. I knew I needed help and support, so I angled to get it whatever way I could. From the first. I was desperate."

"From the first?" he asked blankly. "You were weeping by

the husk of your house. All I did was extend a hand."

"I was distraught, yes, but not unconscious. I saw you were a man. I flashed you with my legs."

Abner felt his jaw fall. "I thought that was accidental."

"Such things are seldom truly accidental. Then when you helped me up, I stepped into you and embraced you, pressing my torso against yours. Making you want me. That was an unfair ploy."

"You wanted me to take you home!" he said.

"I was shameless. I used you. Once I was in your house, I did everything I could to make you want to keep me."

"Because you had nowhere else to go," he said.

"Yes. Today I am sure Pariah will have some sort of placement for me, and I am ready to go. But I would prefer to remain here with you. This is a function of my continuing desperation. I needed you to know, before making my pitch."

"Your pitch?"

"So you understand just how cynical it is, at the root. Like selling a new product by amending it with bangles to evoke a desire despite its uselessness. I want to stay, and I believe I can make it worth your while, one way or another. But I can't take it further without being sure you understand exactly how you are being manipulated. It wouldn't be right."

"Manipulated," he repeated, bemused.

"Including the sex. I played you the way a woman plays a man. But fair is fair."

"But I would have helped you without all that! You don't need to vamp me."

She nodded. "I think that is true. I didn't know you well enough, so I couldn't afford to gamble on your decency. I apologize."

He considered her carefully. "Complete cynicism. Like that of a sopath."

She rocked back as if struck. "Dear God, you're right! I hate that. I don't deserve any more of your courtesy. Let's go see Sylvia. She should have advice for me, where to stay while my identity gets sorted out."

He felt abruptly guilty. Was she still playing him? "No, wait. I haven't heard your pitch."

"You want to hear it now?"

"Yes. You strike me as a woman who knows what she wants and goes efficiently after it. What you have to say is bound to make sense."

"Then bear with me a moment." She got up and went to the downstairs bathroom. He heard her sobbing. Oh—another siege of grief. He knew exactly how that was.

Soon she emerged, her face repaired.

"I'm sorry," he said. "It was an unkind analogy. I said it without thinking."

"It was an accurate one. That's what got me. I was acting like a sopath. I can't blame you for being turned off."

"The pitch," he reminded her tersely.

"It is this: I need you, because I have no resources at the moment. I am ready to do what is required to make you satisfied to have me remain here."

"Yes, you demonstrated that last night."

She made a wan smile. "That, too. You are similarly devastated, and, as you admitted, ill-equipped to handle things like housekeeping, laundry, meals, and shopping. The thousand little things that keep a family going. But you will need to handle them, and keep your health up, because in a few days you will have to return to your job, and do it well. Otherwise you'll lose it, and you'll have one hell of a time getting another. Because of what happened."

She was on target. "I guess I hadn't thought that far ahead."

"I can provide the support you need to function. So you can go to work and pretend that things are normal at home. Because they will be, to the extent I can make them." She gave him a straight look. "I can't offer you the reality, just the illusion. No love, of course. But you won't have to struggle with anything at home. That's worth something."

"It is," he agreed. "The illusion of family."

"And the ordinary details of running the household. It isn't much, but it's all I can offer. It doesn't have to be permanent. Just until we both get better organized. Mutual convenience. A practical matter."

"Let's do it," he said.

"But I thought you--"

"I don't think you're a sopath. I regret saying what I did. Stay. If the sex is a turnoff for you, no need to do it. Your deal makes sense."

"Sex is not a turnoff for me. It's a tool. Part of my arsenal. I don't have a lot of skills, but I'm good at what I do, and that is part of it. You know that it's a service, like the housekeeping. I like doing it well. I feared my realism in this respect would repel you."

"It doesn't. You have skills I lack. You are practical in ways that I am not. You are right: I need you to shore me up in my hour of crisis. You need me similarly. We surely have little in common apart from the horror of our losses, but for now we are good for each other. Until that situation changes, stay here. Please."

"Thank you. I confess to being strangely drawn to you, apart from the mutual convenience."

He smiled. "Women tend to be drawn to me. I don't know why, but more than one at work has hinted that she would be available if I were interested. Of course I have not taken advantage of them."

She gazed at him with an indefinable expression. "May I kiss you?"

He realized that for her such a kiss was more significant than sex, despite kissing having become part of their sexual interaction, because it signaled her true feeling. The fact that she asked was similarly significant. She was signaling its importance to her.

He stood up. "Let's kiss each other."

She stood and joined him. They kissed. She was firm and yielding, fitting herself perfectly to him, and her lips seemed to

41

be on fire. His desire was rekindled, as perhaps she intended. Yet he felt the first spark of something that would challenge their agreement that there was no real love in their relationship.

CHAPTER 3

They went together to Sylvia's house. She was busy trying to calm two children. "They're just in," Sylvia said. "Police brought them. Two different families. Both freaked out."

"Maybe we can help," Abner said.

Sylvia became fully aware of him. "Yesterday—you took the woman home."

"Me," Bunty agreed. "We worked it out."

The little girl was about five, with a wild tangle of dark hair. She looked startlingly like Bunty. She took one look at Abner and ran to him.

He picked her up and held her, and she cried into his chest. Again, what else could he do?

Meanwhile Bunty went to the boy, who was about six. She put her arms about him and kissed the top of his tousled blond head. He too dissolved into tears.

"You seem to have the touch, both of you," Sylvia said. "Do you want to take them home?"

Startled, Abner exchanged a glance with Bunty. She nodded.

Thus suddenly and simply, they were driving home with the two children strapped into the rear car seats. The children had really chosen them, and they had accepted.

At the house, Bunty took over. "What's your name?" she asked the boy.

"Clark."

"Yours?" she asked the girl.

"Dreda."

"Clark and Dreda, what happened to you was too horrible to talk about. You are here now, and we will take care of you.

We lost our families the same way: sopaths."

"Sopaths!" the girl cried, shrinking away.

"So we understand. We don't blame you. Now how about some chocolate ice cream?"

That got both children's attention. Soon they were eating dishes of it.

"You're a wonder," Abner murmured behind Bunty.

"This is my sphere of expertise," she murmured back.

But both children remained tight after eating and having their faces wiped. "They're afraid to let go," Abner said. "We have to reassure them."

Bunty tried. "It's okay to cry," she told the children.

But they didn't. They had cried before, but not now. "They think they're being adopted out," Abner said. "They don't want to make a bad impression."

"Understandable. But how do we reassure them?"

"I think the nuclear option."

"You have the nerve to try it?"

"I'm not sure. I'll try." He faced the children. "You are each survivors of sopaths. You don't have to tell what happened. But I will explain about us."

The two gazed at him.

He took a breath. "There was a sopath in my family. She killed her brother." He saw the boy wince. He had seen similar. "Then she killed her mother." Both winced. "Then she tried to kill me. I picked her up by the feet and cracked her head into a wall, and she died. I killed my daughter. I hate it, but I did. She was a sopath."

Dreda wailed. Then she came to Abner. He picked her up and held her close.

"And I killed my son," Bunty said. "By throwing him in a fire. He was a sopath too."

"I had to do it," Clark whispered.

"Because he was a sopath," Bunty said.

"Yes."

"He tried to kill you."

"I had a knife. I was afraid of him. He was smaller than me, but, but--"

"Merciless," Abner supplied.

"When he tried to stab me, I stabbed him first."

"You had to," Bunty said. "He was a sopath."

Now he cried. She took him in, comforting him.

"It was the same with you?" Abner asked Dreda. "You don't have to answer."

"He tried to—do a bad thing," the girl sobbed.

"He tried to kill you?"

"No. He—he always wanted to see me bare. I wouldn't let him. Mom protected me. But then he killed Mom."

"And you had no more protection," Abner said, trying to control his shudder.

"He had a knife. I was afraid, and took off my dress. He got bare too. He had a—his thing was hard, sticking out. He held me down and tried to put it in me, between my legs."

Her brother had gotten a random erection, and tried to rape her? "How old was he?" Abner asked.

"Seven."

It was possibly normal curiosity. Boys did wonder what was supposed to be special about girls. Maybe the boy had seen a sex video, and tried to emulate it. When he had his erection, and opportunity. "How far did he get?" Abner asked carefully.

"It wouldn't go in. It was too big. He pushed harder. It hurt. I screamed, but he didn't care. He dropped the knife and used his hand to push his thing in. Then it really hurt. I screamed and screamed, but he wouldn't stop. So I grabbed the knife and jammed it into his neck. Then he stopped. There was blood all over. I got away. He died. I killed him."

"That is called self-defense," Abner said.

"But he wasn't trying to kill me. Just to get his thing into me. If I'd let him, he would have gone away. Like when he wanted my candy. If I gave it to him, he went away. He said it was because he liked me. I should have let him put his thing in. But it hurt too bad."

"He tried to rape you," Abner said. "You defended yourself. You were right to do that."

"But if he liked me--"

Abner spoke very carefully. "Sopaths don't like anybody. They only use them. He liked the idea of raping you. Most little boys don't care about sex, but some do. It makes them feel good. Even if it makes the girls feel bad. He was wrong to try. You were right to stop him. Even if he died."

"I was?"

"You were," Bunty agreed. "He said he liked you so you wouldn't fight him. So he could do what he wanted. Because it's hard to do when a girl is fighting it. He was using you."

"He just wanted the candy," Abner said. "Your body was like a kind of candy."

"Little girls are like candy!" Dreda exclaimed.

"In some respects," Bunty agreed, smiling. "And little boys can be like snakes."

Dreda smiled back. The crisis had passed, for now.

Then they remembered Clark. He had heard the whole sequence. That could be mischief.

"You never tried that with a girl, did you?" Abner asked him.

"No," Clark said, horrified. "I knew it was wrong."

"It is wrong for children," Bunty said. "When they grow up, and know what they are doing, and the woman agrees, then it is all right. Then it doesn't hurt."

"So you don't hate me," Dreda said.

"We don't hate you," Abner said. "You did what we all did. You killed a sopath. That's the end of it."

Both children looked relieved.

"Now let me show you your rooms," Bunty said.

"But I don't want to be alone," Dreda protested.

Oops. It was understandable, but could they afford to let the children spend nights with the adults?

Bunty handled it. "Did your folks let you sleep with your parents?"

"No," Dreda said uncomfortably.

"Because they had adult things to do at night, and you needed to learn to sleep by yourself."

"Yes. But then my brother came."

There was the crux. "The sopath."

"Yes. Because he knew I was alone."

There was a potent argument. She had excellent reason not to like being alone. Bunty looked pleadingly at Abner.

"There are no sopaths here," he said. "It is sopaths you fear, not boys."

"Yes."

"Would you share a room with Clark?"

She looked at the boy assessingly. She knew his history was similar to hers. "Yes."

Half there. Abner turned to the boy. "Would you share a room with Dreda? So the two of you are not alone?"

"Yes. I shared with my sister." He squirmed. "I wasn't supposed to peek when she washed. But I did."

Abner smiled. "So did I, when I was small. It's a boy thing."

"A man thing," Bunty said with half a smile.

"Boys peek at girls," Abner said. "Men peek at women. They're interesting. But you can't touch."

"Yes."

"And you pretend not to notice," Bunty said. "And she'll pretend not to peek at you."

Clark was surprised. "Girls peek?"

"We do. But not as much."

"You told!" Dreda reproved her.

Both Abner and Bunty had to repress smiles.

"Not as much?" Clark asked.

"Girls are just more interesting than boys," Abner explained. "So boys peek more. You know that."

The boy nodded, satisfied.

"Dreda is not your sister," Abner concluded. "But for now maybe you should think of her as one."

"You're not my father," Clark said surprisingly.

There was more than one way to interpret that statement. Abner chose the one that fit his purpose. "True. I am not. None of us are related to each other. But you may if you wish think of me as your father, and Bunty as your mother. We are thinking of you as our children. We have all lost our families, and now this is all we have."

"But will you take us back to Pariah tomorrow?"

"No!" Abner said. Then he looked at Bunty.

"No," she agreed. "We are an artificial family. A pretend family. We won't send you away until you want to go."

Thus was another decision made. "We'll go back to Pariah as a family," Abner said. "We will stay together."

Both children relaxed visibly. They had feared being isolated again. Then Dreda came to hug Abner, and Clark hugged Bunty. Abner discovered to his surprise that he was just as relieved as the children were. He dreaded the prospect of being alone with his grief, and this kept him from that.

Bunty set about preparing them for a residence in what had been Jasper's room. Abner sat heavily on the couch, unwinding, continuing his thought. They had become an impromptu family, and he was not dismayed. The children filled a raw hole in his life, as did Bunty. In fact a significant part of it was that this meant that Bunty would remain here indefinitely, playing the role of wife and mother. Running the household, keeping things in order, being company. Giving him sex. He felt guilty acknowledging it, but he did crave it. All of it. Maybe he was in a state of rebound, not just in love, but in the whole family. Still, it felt right.

Bunty and the children reappeared. Clark was dressed in Jasper's clothes, which fit well, they being the same age. Dreda wore more of Jasper's clothes, cinched to fit her smaller frame. Abner looked askance.

"Two things," Bunty said briskly. "Your little girl was three, and Dreda is five, so she's too big for that clothing. And yours was the sopath. We don't want to touch her things."

Poison. He had to agree. Abner spread his hands. "Of course.

You can take Dreda shopping for her own things."

"This afternoon," Bunty agreed. Then she paused. "I will have to borrow some money."

Because she had nothing. "We'll all go. I'll pay for anything we need. Tomorrow we'll see about getting your ID restored so you can function on your own."

"Thank you."

It was in one sense an entirely typical family afternoon with two parents seeing to the needs of two children. In another sense it was refreshingly strange, as the four of them integrated despite their disparate origins. All he had to do was follow Bunty's cues. Abner really appreciated it.

Things ran late, so they stopped at a fast food place for dinner. It was fun.

That night, the children safely in bed, Bunty embraced him and kissed him ardently. "You were wonderful!"

"You were the wonderful one," he said. "You handled everything."

"You supported me completely, and I don't mean just monetarily. You gave me legitimacy."

"You *are* legitimate."

"I'm a lost woman you took in. Then you let me take in the children. You have been more than kind."

He was embarrassed by her gratitude. "Well, you flashed me with your legs. What else could I do?"

"Shut up." She wrapped those legs about him, and they were in the throes of fantastic sex.

"Seriously," she said when it abated. "Can you afford all this? We spent a fair amount of money today, and it promises to continue."

"I have a good job. As long as I keep that, I can afford it."

"You will keep it," she said firmly. "But about the children: you know we can't just throw them back into the water. You and I alone could have split up the moment I got my identity back. But when we took them in, it became more complicated. You had to know that."

"I did know that. But their need was dire. And you—Bunty, I know we agreed not to speak of love, and it will be some time before we come to terms emotionally with our dreadful losses. But I seem to be in the process of rebounding rapidly, and already I care for you more than I should. The children in effect lock you in, and I think that's what I want."

"Romeo and Juliet."

"What?"

"Romeo had just lost his love when he met Juliet. It was rebound."

"And they died!"

"But *we* don't have to. My point is that rebound love is no shame. We have a lot of emotion in flux. We'll never get our original loves back, so we can afford to let it take us."

"But you explained how cynically you played me from the start, to secure your welfare for the moment. Where is your true emotion, Bunty?"

"I did play you," she agreed. "But now I'm looking beyond the moment, and you remain an excellent prospect. I'm in rebound too, Abner. It may not be real, but it feels like nascent love. I won't fight it if you don't. Planned love can work just as well as random love, perhaps better. I think we can make it together. This afternoon was confirmation."

"So you do feel for me."

"I do. I've always been honest with you, and I am being honest now."

It was a confirmation he had desperately needed. "You are about due for your collapse. May I join you in that?"

"Oh, yes."

They lay embraced, and both broke into sobs of grief. It was weirdly refreshing.

And there were the children standing by the bed, alarmed. They had heard the sobbing and came to investigate, being excruciatingly sensitive to family mischief. What could they have thought was happening? That the adults were fighting each other?

"We were making love, the way your parents did," Bunty

told them. "That's why we're bare. But then we remembered."

Abner made a decision. "Just for this hour, join us," he said. "We are crying for our lost families. You lost yours too. Cry with us. It's okay to cry. We all need to express our grief."

The two climbed onto the bed and accepted the nude embraces, pretending not to notice that aspect. They cried with abandon. All of them cried together, supporting each other in this too. It didn't mean that they didn't value their new family, just that they had formidable residual issues to work out emotionally. The fact that they could openly do this surely contributed significantly to their ability to cope.

And Abner, lying there with his arms around the other three, knew that they would never separate as a family.

*

In the morning they went to the administrative offices to see about Bunty's identity. The authorities understood about sopath mischief and facilitated the process, and Bunty emerged with temporary ID that would serve while the wheels ground more slowly for the rest. She wasn't destitute; she was the inheritor of her husband's estate, once it clarified.

"And we need to register the children for school and preschool," Bunty said.

Abner hoped it would be that simple.

"They're not yours," the official pointed out.

"Sopaths. We're an ad hoc temporary family."

"They won't take them. The paperwork's not in order." He held up his hand to forestall her protest. "I know. It's a pretext. They won't take any sopath survivors. They will stall indefinitely. There's a bias, unofficial but powerful. They think those children are killers. You will have to make other arrangements."

"Demonizing the victims," Abner said.

"The new racism," Bunty muttered.

"I didn't say it," the man said, nodding affirmatively. He sympathized, but had given them the reality.

Bunty's mouth was thin as they left the office. "I want to try the schools directly."

Abner shrugged. She had her way of doing things, and he liked her initiative, even if at times it seemed futile.

They went to the grade school Jasper had attended. Classes were changing and the hall was thronged with children.

Dreda clung to Abner's leg, whimpering. He picked her up. "What's the matter, honey?"

"Sopaths," she whispered in his ear.

He froze. "Sopaths here?"

"Two." She shrank again. "Three."

Bunty, overhearing, took Clark's hand. "True?"

"Yes," the boy said.

"You can tell just by looking?"

Both children nodded. It seemed they had become supersensitized, and were able to see what the adults did not.

"Let's get out of here," Bunty said grimly.

Abner agreed. If sopaths were in the regular classes, there would be real mischief soon enough, and it was better to be well clear of it.

"How do you know?" Bunty asked the children as they emerged from the building.

"I can feel their souls," Dreda said. "Same as my folks had, and my brother didn't. Same as you do."

Bunty looked at Clark. "You too?"

"Yes. Souls are sort of soft and nice. Kids who don't have them are bare."

Bunty glanced at Abner. "It must be something a child can tune in to, like learning language. Especially when there's a bad experience with a sopath."

"Yes," Dreda said. "Daddy has a really strong nice soul. It makes me want to be close."

Abner was startled. He had a strong soul?

"There is a masculine magnetism about you, Abner," Bunty said. "I felt it from the outset. It must be the reason for women's attraction to you."

Abner didn't comment. But it would indeed explain a lot.

"What can we do?" Abner asked when they were back in the car. "Children are required to be schooled."

"But those sopaths are like bombs waiting to destroy their classes."

"I know. But what alternative do we have?" Then he answered his own question. "Homeschooling."

"But I would have to do it," Bunty protested. "You have to keep your job."

"True. You can handle it."

"But I told you I'm not smart. I was a grade C student throughout, sometimes by courtesy. I could never be a teacher."

"Sure you can," Clark said confidently. "Teachers don't have to be smart, just tough." He had been in first grade, so knew the score.

"He's right," Abner said. "You just need to be able to handle children, which you obviously can, and the school routine, which you can keep simple. You'll have books for guidance and information."

"But I'm not qualified. It takes years to get a college degree and a teaching certificate, and I never went beyond high school."

"Homeschooling has different standards," Abner said. "I believe parents are automatically qualified. I'll bet the authorities will be only too glad to let us do it, because they don't want to be bothered with sopath survivor children anyway, as we have discovered."

"Do it mommy," Dreda pleaded. "Please."

Bunty worked it out. "I'm not a teacher, but I can learn. I can get books from the library to start."

Abner took her hand, quietly supporting her. She squeezed his fingers appreciatively. They had come to another key decision.

In the afternoon they went to Sylvia's house, where a regular Pariah meeting was scheduled.

"I believe I have found placements for the children," Sylvia said as they entered.

The children clung close to Abner and Bunty. "No," Abner said.

"We're a family," Bunty added. "We are staying together."

"They'll homeschool us," Clark said proudly.

Sylvia considered, evidently not entirely surprised. "You're making a family unit."

"We are," Abner said. "We like each other."

"I must confirm," Sylvia said, nodding. "A necessary formality." She faced Abner. "Do you, Abner, take this woman and these children to be your pro-tem family?"

He liked this formality. "I do."

"Do you, Bunty, take this man and these children ?"

Bunty seemed similarly satisfied. "I do."

"Do you, Clark, take this man and this woman as your for-now parents?"

"I do," Clark said formally, but he was plainly nervous, as if afraid it would all puff away in a moment.

"Do you, Dreda, take this man and woman as your for-now parents?"

"I do." There were tears in the girl's eyes, not of grief but of eagerness.

"And do you two children take each other as siblings?"

"We do," the children said almost together.

"Then by the informal authority of my position with Pariah, before these witnesses, recognizing your mutual need and desire, I declare you to be an ad hoc family. The authorities will not question this."

Abner and Bunty picked up the children and hugged them and each other. The association had hardly been a day and night, but already it seemed hugely significant.

The assembled survivors broke into applause. They understood. It was not a legal family, but it was real. That was what counted.

But there was further business. "The schools won't take the children," Bunty said. "So we want to homeschool them."

"We're setting up a Pariah charter school here," Sylvia said.

"The authorities are quietly facilitating it, providing financing so we can pay teachers. They appreciate our taking the children off their hands. You can homeschool them if you prefer, but this should be easier."

"Would it be all right if I taught them at the school?" Bunty asked. "I'm really not qualified, but I think I'd like to try."

"You're Pariah-qualified," Sylvia said. "You can be our first teacher. We can do it at your house, to start."

"Yes!" Clark and Dreda said almost together.

"Right now it will be just your own kids. But we have the paperwork for the charter school in motion."

"Good enough," Abner said, gratified. He had seen how the police handled sopath survivors, so this was perhaps not surprising. There were an increasing number of sopaths, which meant ever-more victims, and it was surely a problem.

They returned home. "Tomorrow you can return to your job," Bunty said. "I will keep the household running. I'll check the library. You will have to let me use the car. I have my temporary license now."

She would handle all the routine chores. "Thank you." He meant it.

"Thank *you*. You have given us all a home."

"You have made the family." They kissed.

"Oh, yuck," Clark muttered.

"Maybe you can do that stuff privately," Dreda suggested diplomatically.

Then they all laughed.

*

It was another great night. "We're married now," Bunty said. "Informally, in law and emotion, but it's real in what matters. We should celebrate."

"The wedding night," he agreed.

"Two days ago we had completely different lives. Then came the horror. It's as though we are sealing off those old situations and starting fresh, like amnesiacs, only we haven't forgotten."

"We'll never forget."

"I don't feel free to say the L word, but maybe I'm feeling it."

The L word: Love. It was impossible, this soon, but he felt it too. Their hellish experience had shaken them loose from the old ties and made them ready for new ones. "I suspect it is in our future."

"Our near future, dear." She kissed him passionately.

The sex was if anything even better than it had been on prior nights. Bunty was completely released, participating with abandon.

And when it was done, the children were there for the crying session. It seemed it had become an instant tradition. They had to have been listening, waiting for their turn. Well, they were entitled. It was so much better to have love in the family, than mere convenience.

Next morning Bunty and the children dropped Abner off at work, then headed for the library. Abner fit comfortably back into his familiar routine. No one asked any questions, perhaps fearing the answers. It was enough that he was functioning normally. And he was, thanks to Bunty.

He fought against the thought, but the case was increasingly persuasive: Bunty was just as good a wife as Zelda had been. It wasn't that there was anything wrong with Zelda, or that he didn't love her. Bunty was dynamic, a leader, taking him in new directions. And the children—weren't sopaths.

The family picked him up at the end of the work day. The children were full of news. "We learned about numbers!" Clark said. "I can add three and three!"

"Good for you," Abner agreed.

"And we painted," Dreda said. "I made a duck."

"Wonderful," Abner said, meaning it. Because it meant not only that they were learning, and enthusiastic about it, but that Bunty was successful as a teacher. That meant in turn that they would be able to keep the children out of the public schools, avoiding the sopaths.

Things settled in. They attended Pariah meetings regularly, partly to stay in touch, partly to show off their successful integration as a family. Then Sylvia broached the subject to them. "You're homeschooling for now."

"Yes," Abner said. "Bunty is doing a good job of it, too."

"Our application for the charter school is still tied up in bureaucratic paperwork," Sylvia said. "There are other children in need of schooling, and they need it now. They can't get into the regular schools, and many don't want to."

"There are sopaths there," Abner agreed. "The children can spot them more readily than adults can."

"Exactly. The schools have it backwards, rejecting survivors while unwittingly accepting sopaths and refusing to admit their error. It's bureaucratic idiocy, but we're stuck with it. And of course most survivors don't want to put their children at further risk."

"We understand perfectly," Abner said.

"Can you school more children at your house?" Sylvia asked Bunty.

"I'm really not a teacher. I have no certificate, no credits. I just got books from the library, and followed their guidance."

"You *are* a teacher," Sylvia said. "In the same way you're part of a family. It seems you have the touch. I can get immediate authorization for a temporary interim de facto charter school. It won't be official until the paperwork is done, but it can function. The survivor children need you."

Abner saw Bunty wavering. "How many are we talking about?" he asked.

"Six. At the moment."

Abner looked at Bunty. She spread her hands. "I can try. If it's okay with our children."

Clark and Dreda were enthusiastic. "Our own school!" Clark said. "With mom the teacher."

Thus it came to be. Next day six new children, ages five and six, came to join Bunty's class at home. Abner was away at work, but apparently she handled it well enough. She was after all experienced with children, first her own, then theirs.

In fact he learned that night that she felt fulfilled. She was doing something really useful, and she was good at it.

"Clark and Dreda really helped," she said warmly. "The new children were newly freaked by their experiences and tended to be ashamed and not to trust anyone. But Dreda stood up before them and described her own experience, knifing her brother as he tried to rape her. She was remarkably detailed about the way his penis stiffened and where he tried to push it in. Two of the girls had encountered similar attacks, and they shared their memories. Then Clark told of his desperate fight with his brother, and two of the boys had done the same. It really broke the ice."

"What of the other two children?" Abner asked, morbidly curious.

Bunty grimaced. "It's ugly. The boy was attacked and tortured by his older brother, who thought he knew where the key to the lock-box was that contained the family's savings. The sopath held him down by sitting on his face and kept punching him in the body. They were both in their underwear. The torture wasn't very efficient, but it did hurt. Finally the victim managed to wrench his head up and grab the sopath's penis with his teeth. He chewed through the underpants and the flesh of the penis and scrotum, ripping out any flesh he could manage, and didn't dare quit until he almost severed the member. Blood was everywhere. In the end the sopath bled to death. But he had already killed the parents, leaving the boy an orphan."

Abner shuddered. "And the girl?"

"That was a straight killing, or attempt. The sopath girl came after her with a kitchen knife. She dodged to the side, but the knife sliced off her left ear. Blood poured out, fouling the knife, making it hard to hold firmly. In the sopath's confusion she lost focus, and the victim grabbed hold of her hair with both hands and used it as a lever to bash the sopath's face into the bed post repeatedly until her head caved in and she died. It was a messy, desperate fight. I believe it; the girl does have a bandage where her ear should be, and I doubt she could have made up such a story."

Abner remembered his military experience. Desperation was the word. Normal people could get caught up in kill or be killed combat and do things that appalled them in retrospect. "And then she felt guilty for killing her sister," he said.

"Yes. But the other girls reassured her, and the boys reassured the boy and, well, they all melded. They all understand, and all know they understand, and they feel halfway comfortable at last, at least with each other."

"Then you were able to teach them something."

"Yes. They are actually eager to learn. It's exhilarating."

The semi-formal school started with eight children, including theirs, but in a few days more came in and were similarly integrated. Sopaths were still taking out families. When the number of children passed a dozen, Bunty pleaded for help. Sylvia found another survivor parent who had been a teacher, and she really helped. But children kept coming. They took over a local empty warehouse and converted it into a four room, three teacher school.

Then something quietly amazing happened. A non-Pariah neighbor requested admittance for her young child. It was, she explained, convenient because they lived in the next block, and the word was that it was a really good school that the children liked. She was nervous about their regular school; there were some vicious children there, merciless bullies, and she wanted to take her boy out.

"Sopaths," Bunty murmured. "They would be bullies."

They took the boy, and a few others as they came. They had to expand to four teachers, then five. But it was working, in part because they had virtually no disciplinary problems. The Pariah children knew when they were well off, and the non-Pariah children knew they were there by sufferance. But mainly, Abner knew, it was Bunty. She was really good with children.

Bunty was constantly busy, but she radiated satisfaction. She had found her ideal situation.

One Sunday, by mutual agreement, Abner and Bunty dressed formally and took the children to the local church Abner had attended with his original family. He was not a religious man, but he believed in community participation, and felt this would be a stabilizing influence.

The pastor intercepted him at the entrance and drew him aside. The man had literally seen him coming, having evidently been alert. "Mr. Slate, I will be blunt. We don't want you here."

"I don't understand." But he feared he did. It was like the situation at schools and day-schools. He had been tainted by the sopaths.

"You have taken up an immoral lifestyle we cannot condone here."

Or was it something else? "Be specific."

"You are living with a woman who is not your wife, and exposing two innocent children to this sinful lifestyle."

"My wife was killed by a sopath! So was her husband. And the children's parents. We are trying to survive."

"You are not married to each other," the pastor said.

"We *are* married. Not in a church, true, but we had a ceremony."

"As illicit convenience." The man took a breath. "Privately, I understand your position. The situation with the sopaths is an utter horror. But the church does not. I have expressed its position. Please do not make this more difficult."

Abner saw that there was no recourse here. By the church's dogma, they were living in sin. "Thank you," he said curtly, and returned to his family.

Bunty could tell by his bearing what the news was. She took the children's hands and turned away from the church, physically, emotionally, and socially.

"We understand," Clark said, fighting back tears. "They don't want us."

"We're pariahs," Dreda agreed.

How apt the name was! "We'll form our own church," Abner said resolutely. "Or at least a small non-denomination Pariah service."

"We have done it with the school," Bunty agreed.

They did, using the school premises, and a number of Pariahs and their children attended. They arranged to take turns emulating the type of service: Protestant, Catholic, Jewish, Muslim, and even Atheist. Always they stressed their unity as Pariahs, supporting each other regardless of their several religions. It worked surprisingly well, because all the Pariahs were discovering similar rejection.

The insurance company tried to balk on paying for the loss of Bunty's house. Their stated reason: it was arson, which wasn't covered.

"Corporations are sopaths," Abner muttered. "They have no souls, by definition."

"What can we do?"

"We can get a lawyer."

They did. The lawyer sent a terse legalistic letter pointing out that a five year old child's action was legally considered an accident. The company yielded, evidently realizing that its bluff had failed.

The money, after paying off the mortgage, was not great, but it was much better than nothing. Bunty put it toward the operating expense of the school, and their personal savings.

Authorization as a charter school came though, and the teachers started getting paid. That completed it for Bunty, as she confessed during almost savage lovemaking that night. She had a profession, she loved it, and was satisfied she was doing good for the world.

Abner was satisfied too, as his grief for his original family faded and was overwritten by the needs and feelings of his new family. His old family could never be restored; none of theirs could. They had a new life, and it was sufficient.

In fact he harbored a dark suspicion that his new family was better than his old one, and not just because of their common bond in the horror of the sopaths. It had been assembled mostly by chance, but Bunty was one beautiful and fine woman, and the children were wonderful. Maybe the sopath experience had significantly matured all of them, making them better people. There was surely an element of desperation; they truly needed each other. But he thought it was mainly luck: they were right for each other.

One evening Bunty had a question for him. "My pill prescription is running out. Should I stop taking them?"

She was asking whether they should have a baby together. Abner realized that he would like that. They were careful about speaking of love, as each remained in grief for the lost spouse, but their rebound continued and it felt a lot like a permanent commitment. But he had one ugly thought. "It could be a sopath."

"I'll renew the prescription," she said, shuddering.

So they were at peace with the new order, and life was reasonably good, considering.

Yet the sopath menace would not fade, and it was growing. That meant that their paradise was bound to be temporary.

CHAPTER 4

Bunty called him at work, near quitting time. "Abner, there's a sopath with a gun in the neighborhood. He took a shot at one of the school children. He missed, and the child made it to the house. But the sopath is still out there, I think laying siege to the house, hoping to steal candy or money from the children. I don't dare release school until I know it's safe."

"I'll try to flush him out," Abner said.

"Honey, be careful. I know he's a child, but that gun--"

"I have one too," he reminded her. He had gotten a license, and now carried it at all times, along with a combat knife. Bunty had similar weapons, and they were training the children. It was a matter of survival. So far they hadn't had to use them, but they knew the time would come. With the sopath threat, they had to be ready to fight instantly. That was another thing normal folk tended not to understand. Not until they encountered their own sopaths.

"Don't hesitate."

There was the problem. He would have to go gunning for a child. Could he actually pull the trigger, even if the sopath was firing at him? He thought he could, but had not yet done it. "I'll handle it," he said, hoping that was true.

He phoned the police station. "This is Abner Slate. There's a sopath in my home neighborhood. I'm going to try to take him out."

"We'll send a cruiser." No questions; they knew him, knew of the charter school, and understood the situation. The police could not go gunning for children, but they were becoming supportive of those who went after sopaths.

Abner stopped to buy a huge candy cane that would be visible for a block, a wicked temptation for any child. That was the thing about the sopaths: they were children, the great majority under age six, with the impulses of children. Candy was their chief obsession, and they could and did kill for it, having no scruples.

He parked a block from his house, drew his loaded pistol with his right hand, and held the candy cane aloft with his left. He knew better than to park close to the house and be distracted and exposed when emerging from the car. He walked slowly toward his yard, keeping his head straight so that the sopath would not realize that he was looking around. He saw the police car pausing on a side street.

Where was the most likely hiding place? The bushy hedge that marked the boundary between his front yard and the neighbor's yard. Did he see a bit of color there?

Something moved. Now he saw the glint of the barrel of a pistol as it oriented on him. He jumped to the side as the gun fired, then fired back, aiming carefully.

The sopath's bullet missed him. The child did not know how to aim well or to brace properly for the recoil. Abner's bullet scored. There was a cry from the bush.

Abner sheathed his pistol and stood where he was as the police cruiser approached. They had of course seen the action, heard the shots, and knew that the child had fired first. It was technically self-defense.

The sopath was dead. Abner had scored on the head.

The police took away the small body without comment. Abner had done the job they could not legitimately do, killing an armed and dangerous person. There would be no report.

The door opened and Bunty hurried out. She flung herself into his arms. She had been watching too.

They walked together to the house. The children were at the door. "Daddy killed the sopath," Bunty announced. "Now it is safe outside."

The schoolchildren exited and walked toward their homes,

which were not far distant. They understood all too well. They would tell their adoptive families, who would also understand.

Only when they were safely inside with their own two did Abner collapse. "I killed a child!" he moaned, overwhelmed. He had remained silent in significant part because of horror. A sopath had tried to kill him, and he had killed the sopath. He was a killer, again. He had done what he had to do, but now that it was done and he could relax, he was appalled.

Clark took his right hand, and Dreda his left hand. Bunty kissed him. "You had no choice," Bunty said. "We knew that from the start."

He hoped they were right, but he needed convincing. "Maybe I could have disarmed him."

"Then what?" Clark asked. "Let him go to kill someone else?"

"Leave him to rape someone?" Dreda asked.

They were right. The sopath could indeed have killed someone else, and even as a child, as Dreda knew so well, he could have molested a terrorized girl. The sopath had had to be killed. But Abner still hated the necessity. "There has to be a better way."

"Let's figure that out now," Bunty said. "Clark, didn't you have an idea?"

"Sure. Dump them in a cellar."

"They would just climb out," Abner said, intrigued by the boy's participation. Actually it was hardly surprising, because the children had had thorough experience with sopaths.

"A deep cellar," Clark said. "Locked."

"Then we'd have to feed them."

"Why?"

"Because they may be sopaths, but we aren't. We can't simply imprison children and let them starve. We have to treat them decently. Otherwise we're no better than they are."

The two children exchanged a glance. This was a new concept to them. Slowly they nodded, assimilating it. Souled folk did not act like unsouled folk.

"Feed them candy," Dreda said. "Enough for one."

"They'd kill each other for it," Abner protested.

Dreda just looked at him.

Bunty whistled appreciatively. "Girl, you have a deadly little mind!"

"I learned from our sopath." The one who had destroyed her family.

Abner considered it. Two sopaths confined together. Candy enough for one. There would be only one survivor in short order. Especially if the two had knives.

"We wouldn't have to kill them ourselves," Abner said.

"But we would be setting them up for it," Bunty said. "Unless--" She broke off thoughtfully.

"Unless we gave them enough food for both," Abner said. "So they could share, as normal children would."

"Sopaths don't share," Clark said.

"Exactly," Bunty agreed. "We set them up for peaceful coexistence. But they fight anyway, because greed has no limits. We could put any number in that cellar, with a mountain of food for them all, and only one would remain. Our hands would be relatively clean."

Abner shook his head. "The line between ethics and cynicism becomes obscure."

The children looked blank. "He means it's hard to tell right from wrong," Bunty translated.

"Awful hard," Dreda agreed. "But we're learning."

"What about the bodies?" Abner asked.

"Put them in the sewer," Clark said.

"That leads to the fertilizer processing plant," Bunty agreed. "No mess."

"The police would know," Abner said.

"And pretend not to," Dreda said. She was a sharp study on pretense.

They worked it out, and soon had a plan to present to Pariah. Abner's horror receded. Faced with an implacable foe, they were doing what was necessary, ugly as it was. He doubted he would ever be entirely at ease with it, but it did seem to be the most viable of nasty alternatives.

It came to pass. There was a deserted house in the neighborhood with a large deep cellar with barred windows. It even had a toilet and shower stall. They set it up with bunks, cushions, and blankets. It would do as a detention chamber. Now all they had to do was use it.

They set up a neighborhood watch, with special attention at the times the charter school children were coming and going. They checked any strange children, verifying identification with survivor children, who had extremely sharp senses with respect to sopaths. They set up honey traps baited with candy that the regular children knew to stay away from.

And the sopaths came. They cruised the streets, looking for things to steal, trying to avoid adults. Experience had shown them that adults tended to interfere, and it was easier simply to sneak in when they weren't looking, snatch the candy, and run. But now more sopaths were armed, mostly with knives, some with guns, and they were getting better at using them. They had to be handled carefully.

"It would be easier simply to shoot them," Abner said morosely.

"We go to extraordinary lengths to salvage a portion of our conscience," Bunty said. "Is it worth it?"

"Maybe not. But for me, at this point, this is the way it has to be."

An alarm went off. A nearby trap had been sprung. Abner hurried to the site in time to see the child running from it, carrying the bucket of candy. The sopath could have escaped, had he dropped the bucket, but he was emotionally incapable of doing that. Abner caught him, using thickly padded gloves. "Fight me, and I'll bash you into a tree," he warned.

The sopath decided not to fight. He was a black-haired urchin about six. Abner carried him to the cellar and locked him in, not bothering to check for weapons. He felt a twinge of guilt for that; he was enabling the inevitable. "I will bring food," he said.

"Fuck you," the sopath said.

When he returned, another Pariah, Gomez, had brought in a second boy, a towhead, and was holding him outside the cellar. They needed two people to work it: one to back off the first sopath and open the gate, on guard, the other to shove the second sopath in.

Abner set down the meal, then drew his pistol. "You know what this is," he told the black-haired sopath.

"It's a gun, shithead," the boy said disdainfully. "I want it."

"Stay on the far side of the cell," Abner said. "If you move, I will shoot you."

The boy stayed on the far side, not calling his bluff, which was just as well. Abner unlocked the gate and opened the door with his left hand, never letting the pistol wander from its target. Gomez shoved the towhead in, then lifted the tray of food and set it in too, on the floor.

Abner closed and locked the gate. He holstered the pistol. "Now you may eat," he told the boys. "There is enough for both of you, so you can share."

Both started toward the food, then paused, eying each other. "Mine," the black-haired boy said. He was the larger of the two.

"Yeah?" the towhead asked disdainfully. He drew a small knife.

But the towhead had misjudged the proximity of the black-haired boy. The first boy lunged into him, grabbing for the knife. He dislodged it, and it went skittering across the floor.

The black haired boy had similarly misjudged the tenacity of the tow. The smaller boy, evidently an experienced fighter, rammed into him with a head-butt that knocked the wind out of him. He fell back, gasping, with the tow on top. There was no hesitation; the tow reached for his face and poked a stiffened finger into his right eye, hooking it gruesomely out.

The black hair screamed in pain and shock, but did not give up the fight. He reached up, caught the tow by the hair, and hauled his face roughly down to his own. The black hair opened his mouth and bit the tow's nose. It was no token effort; blood spurted as the black hair wrenched his face from side to side, ripping off the nose. It was the tow's turn to scream in pain.

In the moment the tow's concentration faltered, the black hair heaved him over and rolled on top of him. He grabbed the tow by the hair on both sides and lifted his head, then smashed it down against the floor. He lifted and smashed again, and again, as hard as he could, until finally the tow stopped struggling. He was unconscious or dead.

The black hair got off him, his right eyeball dangling by the nerve cord. He found the lost knife. He picked it up, returned to the tow, and stabbed him repeatedly in the face and neck. Now there was no question: he was dead.

Only then did the black hair seem to feel the full impact of his pain. He fell down against the wall and screamed.

Abner looked at Gomez. The other turned his face aside and vomited. It had been such an absolutely vicious fight, completely unnecessary. Because sopaths didn't share.

Abner drew his pistol again, aimed carefully, and shot the surviving boy through the head. This was not an execution so much as a mercy killing.

"I thought I could handle it, but I can't," Gomez said. "I'll finish my shift tonight, but you'll need someone else tomorrow."

"I understand," Abner said. "I don't like it much myself." Bile was rising in his throat.

They made sure both boys were dead, then hauled them to the sewer pipe and shoved them in.

The second night a solid red-haired Pariah woman joined Abner. She was Maxine, Gomez's ad hoc wife, evidently the tougher of the pair. She accompanied him as they checked the honey traps. They were of different types; some pits, some closed cages, some merely candy that was securely anchored so that a child would have to let it go in order to flee. Like monkeys, sopaths had difficulty ever letting go.

The signal brought them to one with a sopath girl who glared menacingly at them from the closed metal cage. She was unkempt and dirty, with wild brown hair, like a feral cat. "Leave me alone!" she said.

"Are you hungry, honey?" Maxine inquired. "We're going to take you to a prison cell with a good meal."

"Don't touch me, bitch!"

"Or you can stay here," Maxine concluded. She and Abner made ready to leave.

"I'll go," the girl said quickly.

"Then we'll have to cuff you for the trip. Put out your hands."

The sopath hesitated, then slowly put them out. Maxine applied the soft plastic handcuffs. Then Abner opened the cage and released the girl.

She tried to bolt for freedom, but Maxine still had hold of the cuffs and restrained her. Maxine had evidently thought this process through, and was doing an excellent job.

They drove the girl to the Heller Cellar, as a Pariah wag had put it, and locked her in, alone. "We'll fetch the food," Maxine said. "Meanwhile catch yourself a nap."

They checked the other traps, and found another girl, this one a filthy blonde. They took her in, pausing along the way at Maxine's house, where she fetched a package of sandwiches and chocolate milk. The sopath eyed them, drooling.

"The gamines tend to be hungry," Maxine remarked. "Homeless because they're runaways, having to scour garbage cans and try to steal from stores." She glanced at the girl. "You'd be better off reforming and going home, honey."

"Go fuck yourself in the asshole, bitch."

They came to the cellar. The first sopath was lying on the back bunk, evidently asleep. Abner unlocked the gate while Maxine released the cuffs and pushed the girl through. Then she put in the food package. "There's enough here for the both of you," she said per the formula. "Just be nice and share."

The blonde drew her knife and quietly stalked the sleeping girl, not about to give her the slightest chance to wake and compete for the food. She stabbed down viciously. But at that moment the other moved, striking with her own knife. Neither wound seemed to be lethal, but now they were in combat, stabbing each other repeatedly.

It was over within a minute. Both girls collapsed. Now their wounds looked mortal, and in any event both would soon bleed to death. The food was untouched. All because sopaths wouldn't share, again.

They gave it time, to be sure. "I'll dispose of the bodies," Abner said at last.

"I'll clean up the mess," Maxine said, fetching bucket, mop, and scrub-brush.

"We make a good team," Abner said grimly.

"We do," Maxine agreed. She smiled in a manner that hinted she would be amenable to more than a work relationship, were he interested. He ignored it.

The third night they caught another boy.

As luck would have it, another neighbor was bringing in another sopath, a girl, a screaming hellion. "One of each," Maxine remarked. "This should be interesting."

That gave Abner another twinge, but a sopath was a sopath regardless of gender, and it was clear that the girls were as vicious as the boys. Abner hated to admit it, even to himself, but he was curious whether there would be a difference.

They put her in with the boy and Abner went to fetch the food, it being his turn. When he returned, Maxine was gone, a note in her place: emergency at home, she would return soon. Abner suspected that she did not want to witness what happened. Abner found that perversely reassuring: she was not really all that tough, and he was not alone in his guilt.

"There is enough here for both of you," Abner said as he passed the food through the bars. "All you have to do is share."

The children had ignored each other. Sopaths didn't care about sopaths any more than about souled folk. But the arrival of the food changed that. That was tangible, and they were hungry. Both dived for it, and neither would back off. In a moment they were savagely fighting each other. The boy flung his arms around the smaller girl and hurled her away from the food. But she stabbed him in the gut as she went, using a concealed knife, and he sank to the floor, bleeding. She calmly stepped in and slit his throat. Then, as he bled to death, she ate the choicest morsels.

Abner watched through the bars, appalled again by the complete lack of conscience of a sopath. The girl was about six, with curly red hair, a rather pretty child, relatively clean and well-dressed. She had to have a family home, as she was no street urchin.

"Back off," Abner said when she finished. "I have to remove the body."

She looked at him, seeming to become aware of him as a person. "Let me go," she said.

"I can't do that," Abner said uneasily. "Now go to the far side of the cell. I will kill you if you come toward me or try to escape." He hated the fact that it was not a bluff. He would do what he had to do, if she forced the issue. A sopath was a sopath; it was an illusion to think that it was worse to kill a girl than a boy.

"You're a sopath survivor," she said.

"I am."

She moved to the far wall and stood facing away. She evidently understood the protocol. He unlocked the gate, put his hands on the small body, and hauled it out, never taking his eyes off the girl. If she moved, he would drop the body and whip out his knife, striking without pause.

She didn't move. He relocked the gate.

He dragged the body outside and left it there for the moment. He returned to the cell. The girl had turned around and was standing beside the bunk. She looked neater than before;

she must have redone her hair, washed her face and hands, and straightened out her dress. "You should be all right for the night," he said.

She shook her head. "Not here." She peered at him appraisingly. "I'll trade. Let me go and I'll give you a nice fuck."

Abner was shocked despite his awareness of her nature. "You're a child!"

"I'm a sopath. We do what we choose. I know how."

"You can't be serious." Why was he even talking with her? He knew there was no chance of giving her a conscience.

She lay on the bunk, lifted her skirt, and spread her legs. She wore no panties; she must have removed them when cleaning up. She put her hands to her hairless cleft and drew the vulva lips apart to show her open vagina. "You have to let me put your cock in my cunt for you, slowly, so it stretches and doesn't hurt. Once it's in, then let it spout. Or I can suck it. I promise not to scratch or bite. Or use my knife; you can disarm me first, once we agree on terms. That's easier."

It was evident that she knew what she was offering. She had had sex with a man, maybe more than one, in more than one manner. Abner was horrified, yet also morbidly intrigued. How could she have come by such experience? "No."

But she persisted. "It isn't as if you're doing it with a real girl. I'm a sopath. I won't tell."

"As if a sopath could ever be trusted!"

She laughed. "Got me there, handsome. But I won't tell if it's worth it to me not to, so you can trust that. I never told before, because it would be bad for business."

"We have no such business."

She spread her legs a little wider. "You can put it in my ass if you like that better; there's more room in there." She licked a finger and poked it into her rectum.

He averted his gaze, as much to mask his burgeoning horror as from any modesty, and tried to change the subject. "How old are you?" Her dialogue and action seemed too cynically mature for her appearance.

"Seven. I'm small for my age. But I know what's what. Some men like to fuck little girls." She smiled winsomely. "Try it; maybe you'll like it."

"I'll never like such an abomination! I'm not into children."

"Yet. Doesn't my cute little cunt give you a hard-on?"

"No!"

"Yeah? Show me your pecker, then. I'll bet it's swelling."

"Your attitude revolts me. Are you trying to make me kill you?"

That got to her, because she realized that he could kill a sopath. She drew down her dress. "So what do you want?"

He tried again to change the subject. "You were kicking and screaming when you were brought in. Why are you so calm now?"

"I can behave when I have reason. I do it all the time, at home and school. Throwing a tantrum didn't work. Offering a fuck didn't work. Maybe being reasonable will."

She was smart. That made him uncomfortable in another manner. "You're still a sopath."

"And you're a souler. That doesn't mean we can't deal."

He had to cut this short. "I'll bring more food in the morning."

She rolled off the bunk and to her feet. "You have to let me go. I've been out too long. Mom will worry."

"What do you care about your mother's concern? You're a sopath. Sopaths don't care about the feelings of others."

"I care because it directly affects my welfare. I'm not stupid; I'm damn smart. My IQ test didn't show it because I knew smart could be dangerous, so I faked a few wrong answers. But I knew all the answers." She paused, considering. "Except one. What does DMZ stand for?"

"Demilitarized Zone. It's where neither side brings weapons or sets up military installations."

"You must be smart to know that."

"No. I was in the military. It's the kind of thing you pick up."

She shook her head cannily. "Maybe so, but you are smart. I like that." She peered at him. "There's something about you. Maybe it's your strong soul."

Her insight made him nervous. "This is not about me. You were trying to talk me into letting you go."

"Yes. I'm smart. In fact I'm the bastard child of Mom's affair with a genius. Dad doesn't know, and I sure as hell won't tell him and break up the family. I know how to behave like a souler, and I do it at home so my folks don't catch on."

"Then why spill such secrets to me, a stranger?"

Again that assessing look. "You're not really a stranger, Abner Slate. I know about you."

He was startled. "How do you know my name?"

"This is my neighborhood. I looked at a city chart. I have eidetic memory. I can name your whole artificial family. I know how you've been snagging sopaths and killing them."

He was startled again. "How could you fall into our traps, then?"

"You're cute and smart and you keep your word. I wanted to get to know you, find out your secret. Maybe fuck you."

"You *wanted* to--" He retrenched, realizing that she was baiting him. "You put your life at serious risk because you think I'm cute? That's not smart."

"I can escape when I want to. But I want you to let me go. It's better that way. Maybe if I smile and say please, just like a real girl?"

Abner's uneasiness increased. "I still can't let a sopath go."

She eyed him yet again with that disturbing assessment. "What's your price?"

"No price," he said as he turned to leave.

"There's always a price. If not a fuck, maybe information? I'll make it worth it."

"What information could you possibly have that would justify my releasing a sopath?"

"Like maybe who else likes child fucking. Some respectable family men. Even some policemen."

That made him pause. "I don't believe it."

"Then you're being a fool. I can tell you things to save your life. You trust the police? Don't."

"Why not?" He knew this was treacherous ground, but he couldn't let it go.

"Because they're using you to do their dirty work. I bet they have a dossier on you, to convict you of murder, if you ever cross them. They are like sopaths. Some of them have pretty thin souls."

She had a fairly adult vocabulary when she chose to use it. He was getting to know her, and that made him reluctant to condemn her. "How can you know this?"

"Would you trust a policeman who fucks a child? My ass could tell such stories!"

Abner was sickened, but what she said made awful sense. The police had been phenomenally cooperative, letting Pariah do the sopath-killing for them. Yes, they needed to be rid of sopaths. But a dossier would indeed be a deadly legal weapon. This was something he needed to discuss with Pariah.

"And I think there are some grown sopaths," she continued, orienting on his interest like the little predator she was. "Teen, anyway. Not many, but some. Maybe some older yet. They got through before the type was identified. Spies, assassins, slaughterhouse workers, mercenaries, politicians, corporation bosses. They're good at what they do, because they're smart and have no scruples, like me."

Again it rang distressingly true. "Who are you?" he demanded.

"Call me Nefer. I'm in a regular family. They don't know, as I said, because I behave when I'm with them. It's an effort. Sometimes I just have to get out and be myself for a few hours. I usually sneak out at night when they think I'm in bed, but I can't afford to stay out too long or they'll catch on. I got tempted and let you catch me. I won't do that again. Now let me go; I've paid a fair price."

Abner realized that he was no longer capable of killing her. She had made him sympathize with her, exactly as she intended. And she had provided him with useful insights. Nefer was eerily intelligent in a way he had not realized any child could be. She was a sopath, but he had to honor the deal he had somehow tacitly made.

He sighed. "You have given me things to think about. It does seem only fair that I make the trade." He unlocked the gate and opened it. Would she attack him the moment she was able to? If she did, he would be able to do the right thing and kill her.

But she didn't. She stepped out and paused. "We'll stay in touch, Abner."

He was surprised. "I thought you'd get far away from here."

"No, as I said, this is my territory. Where my contacts are. You're a contact now."

"Why would I ever want to be that?"

"For information. We'll trade. I may need your help some time. I'll pay, one way or another."

Abner considered, and realized that this was an appalling but valid offer. He was making a deal with a sopath, who would pay with information. "With luck we'll never meet again."

Nefer shrugged. "I'm sorry we didn't fuck. It might have been fun with you. It's usually such a chore. You're a good man, like my dad, only more savvy. I kinda like you. I'd kiss you if you let me."

"I won't let you!" he exclaimed, appalled once more. Was the power he held over females extending even to a seven-year-old? Who had perhaps sought him out for that reason?

She smiled. "Not tonight. But maybe sometime."

"Never! Now go away."

"One more thing. I said I could escape. You thought I was bluffing."

"I did."

"Watch. Say that bunk is you behind the bars, when we were talking."

"I don't see what—"

She drew her knife and hurled it. It sailed neatly through

the bars and wedged into the mattress.

Abner was amazed. She could indeed have struck him with her thrown knife, possibly killing him. She truly had held off because she wanted to talk with him. She was the most dangerous kind of sopath: one with self-control.

She recovered her knife. "But I wanted to make you release me, so we could have a relationship. Don't forget to get rid of the body." Then she was off into the night.

Abner was disturbed anew by her boldness. But he had to admit to himself that one reason he had let her go was that their dialogue had caused her to become a person to him, and he couldn't cold-bloodedly kill a person. Not even, as it turned out, a sopath.

This time he chose a different method of disposal. He dragged the boy's body to his car, wrapped it in a tarpaulin, and drove to the city dump, which was closed for the night. He heaved it onto a pile of garbage, where it would get buried by the next load. If the garbage workers saw it, they would keep quiet, knowing it was a sopath.

Witnessing a killing, and disposing of the corpse, were awful things. But his dialogue with Nefer was worse.

Back home, he talked with Bunty, who brought in the children and made it a family discussion. The idea of shielding children from the realities of life and death was foolish under the circumstances. "Maybe it's right, daddy," Dreda said. "The sopaths are getting harder to spy, and some may pass as soulers. I can only be really sure if I touch one, which I hate to do. We need to know more about them."

"But she—she tried to seduce me," Abner said. "Her vocabulary, her actions were gross."

"They do use sex," Dreda reminded him. "It's just a tool to them, and some of them like it." As of course she knew from her own experience.

"But this business about the police," Bunty said. "That's alarming. I fear they do have dossiers on us. We should have thought of that before."

"So the sopath maybe saved us from some real trouble," Clark said.

"It was right to let her go," Dreda concluded.

"Maybe," Abner agreed reluctantly.

They shared the warning with Pariah, who concluded that they would have to stop letting the police pick up the bodies. The option Abner had chosen might also be suspect. The sewer disposal option became the first choice. They would feed future bodies into the pipe.

The nocturnal sopath killings continued. The children slaughtered each other, but Abner didn't deceive himself: he was setting it up, and was responsible for their deaths. He was getting used to it, but it still appalled him.

"One thing bothers me especially," Maxine said one evening as they loaded the bodies for disposal. "Children are young, and it takes them time to develop consciences. Suppose we are killing some who do have souls, but haven't grown into them yet, as it were?"

Abner suffered a horrendous revelation. "Ultimately, it doesn't matter. If we kill a sopath, he's gone. If we kill a souler, his soul is returned to the bank, as it were, and is available for the next birth, which would otherwise have been a sopath."

"That's sickening!"

"But true."

"But true," she agreed. "It doesn't make me feel better about it."

"I don't feel better either," he agreed. "I hate every aspect of this business. But what else can we do? Any sopath we don't kill is bound to kill someone else before long."

"That's the cold equation," she agreed morosely. "Some of the sopaths are actually returning souls to the pool, that way, ironically."

Another day, Saturday, Abner and the family were at the grocery store. Bunty normally shopped alone, but on the weekend the others liked to express their preferences. They were still getting comfortable as a family, rounding off edges.

Abner froze. There ahead of them were a woman and a girl. He knew the child. Nefer! With her mother.

They turned to go down the next aisle. Nefer glanced his way and smiled, exactly like a nice normal girl. She recognized him! But she gave no other sign.

Then they were gone, and Abner's party was in another aisle. He remained bemused.

Dreda took his hand. "You saw something, daddy."

He had to tell the truth. "The sopath," he murmured.

She pursed her lips, imitating one of Bunty's expressions. "I didn't know. She's good." She meant good at masking her nature.

Back in the car he had to tell the others. "I saw Nefer, the sopath I freed."

"Her mother doesn't know," Bunty said.

"She doesn't. The child's an actress."

"So they are learning to emulate normals," Bunty said. "That's dangerous."

"Yes. I shouldn't have released her."

"You made a deal, dad," Clark said. "Soulers honor their deals."

"I hope we don't all come to regret it."

A few days later, as Abner went out in the morning for his drive to work, a voice spoke from the back seat. "Abner."

He recognized it. "Nefer! What are you doing in my car?"

"You left it unlocked. Don't do that again. If I'd been a hostile sopath, you'd be dead."

She was right. He would be scrupulous in that regard hereafter. "What do you want?"

Nefer scrambled over the seat to join him in front, in the process managing to give him a glimpse of her pantyless crotch. He knew it was deliberate, because she was holding her panties in her hand. "Tomorrow you're taking your family to the fair."

That was true. The traveling fair was in town, and promised to be fun for the children. She could readily have guessed. "So?"

"I want to go with you. My folks aren't going. I want to see the sights, eat cotton candy, ride the rides, play the rigged games. The whole thing."

"You're a sopath!"

"So they won't let me in, if they know. They won't know if I'm with you. No one else will know."

"My family will know!"

"Tell them it's okay. I want to have fun. Just because I'm a sopath doesn't mean I don't like kid fun. I'll trade for it."

It revolted him, but it was feasible. "What do you offer?"

"Tonight a boy sopath is going to ambush you. Between your car and your house. With a gun. As one did before, with the school kids, only this one's after you. To get your wallet, with money. So he can go to the fair. He figures he can pass, if he tries hard."

"How do you know this?"

"He told me. I traded him for half."

"Traded?"

"I gave him a really good fuck. Some boys like that, even if they can't spout. Mostly they're just curious about what's there with a girl, seeing her cunt, poking a finger in, getting a feel of her ass. Juvenile stuff. I've done it for petty cash. But some really do want to do it all the way if they can just figure out how. I knew how to get him hard, and how to get it in. It's easier with a boy my size, and he doesn't spout, so it's fairly clean. He'd never have made it with a souler girl, and another sopath girl would have killed him if he tried. But I made a deal, and delivered. Just as I will with you, when you're willing."

"So why are you telling me?"

"You're a contact. You can be useful. More useful than half your money would be. Anyway, I like you. More than I ever liked a man before."

"Sopaths don't like anybody."

"We're incapable of real friendship, but I like your look, as I said, and there's something about your soul. Maybe it's a passing fancy. I still figure some day you'll fuck me."

"I will not!" Yet now he understood why she thought so. She had seduced grown men before, her way.

"As long as we associate, there's a chance. It could be fun trying, with your big cock, easing it in. I might even get an orgasm with you."

That much he could correct. "A child can't get an orgasm."

"Sure they can. They can't spout, but they can get the feeling. I do it when I stroke my clit long enough and use a vibrator in my cunt. But not with a man. I have to pay too much attention to making his big cock fit in my little hole, and then there's the mess when it spouts, so I don't get the feeling. It's purely business. But you're nice, and I really go for you, and maybe I could get there with you, if you fucked me slowly. If you kissed me and told me how you liked me. My slit gets wet just thinking about it."

He had thought he was beyond shock, but he wasn't. She had set him straight with a vengeance. "No."

"I wish you'd let me try," she said wistfully. "You're the only man I ever wanted it with. You wouldn't even have to make a deal. I'd let you just do it. I'd even like it if you spurted into me, because that would mean it was real. I'd save the gism."

It was past time to change the subject. "So you may have saved my life with your warning about the ambush, and I will have to take you to the fair tomorrow."

"That's it."

What could he do? She had delivered, as before. "Okay. Just don't expect my family to welcome you."

"I don't care about them. I just want the fair."

"But there will have to be some rules for the occasion. Leave the vocabulary behind. In fact, don't mention sex at all."

"I'm a sopath, not a moron, Abner. I'll be a proper innocent girl."

He had to smile, reluctantly. Innocent sopath was an oxymoron, especially in her case. "And if you get mad about something, don't draw your knife or throw a fit. Tell me quietly what's bothering you and I'll try to fix it. That's the civilized way. I don't want a scene."

"You and me both, Abner."

"And don't call be Abner."

She looked sidelong at him. "You'd rather I called you daddy?"

"No!"

"Or lover?"

"No!" he repeated, horrified. But she had a point. "Call me Mr. Slate, just as if you respect me."

"I do respect you, Mr. Slate. That's why I want to be near you."

Was it sarcasm? He wasn't sure. "The way a normal girl would respect the father of one of her friends."

"I know the act. I'll even keep my panties on." She put them back on at this point. "You know why I respect you? I can trust you. Because you do what you think is right, even when tempted. Not all souled folk do that, and none of the sopaths."

"I'm not tempted!"

"You're a man, right? When you see into a girl's split, you want it. All men do."

"I don't!"

She merely smiled. "Let me off at the next stop sign."

He did, and she left the car. She looked exactly like a typical schoolgirl as she walked away. But not only was she a sopath, she had compromised him.

He called Bunty from work to advise her of the deal. "We have to do something about that ambush," he said.

"We'll set up a counter ambush," she said. "You be completely normal."

"That's nervous business."

"Dealing with sopaths is. I don't look forward to tomorrow."

Neither did Abner.

He drove home exactly on schedule. He parked the car and got out.

There was a shot from the bush. He ducked.

"It's okay, dad," Clark called. "I got him."

So he had. There was a dead boy in the bush, shot through the head. Clark had taken out the sopath as he got ready to shoot at Abner.

Then Abner was holding Clark while he cried. He didn't like killing any better than Abner did, though he had killed before.

But the fact remained: Nefer might have saved his life. The sopath might have missed, or Abner might have heard him and dived clear, or Bunty might have seen the boy setting up. But most of the risk had been eliminated by Nefer's warning. She had earned her day with them.

Bunty had gone over it with the children, so they were prepared. They didn't like it any better than Abner or Bunty did, but they were necessary realists. "Just ignore her," Bunty advised.

"We'll pretend she's real," Dreda said bravely.

Next morning Nefer was there by the car, modestly garbed. She took her place in silence.

Abner paid for the five and they entered the fair. He bought cotton candy for all, and paid for the rides and games. Nefer behaved perfectly, which meant acting just like an innocent excited child. She was able to follow rules when she had reason, exactly as she had told him.

When it came to the horror house Clark and Dreda hung back. But Nefer wanted to go. He knew that was why the other two did not want to: they would be jammed in close with the sopath.

Abner hesitated. Bunty would stay with theirs, but that meant he would have to go with Nefer, because children were required to be accompanied by adults. "I don't want to be alone with her," he whispered to Bunty. "You know why."

She did. There was no telling what the sopath would do in the noisy darkness. She might try to kiss him, or get her hand into his fly. She might try for more. She had a vagina she wanted to get into play one way or another, and in the privacy of the horror house the limits might be off. "We'll all go," Bunty decreed.

They all went, carefully seated. Clark and Dreda sat beside Abner, while Nefer sat beside Bunty. That eliminated any chance for any funny business. The sopath did not protest; in fact she almost seemed relieved. Perhaps because she didn't trust herself not to mess up their deal, if tempted.

And the ride was fun. They all enjoyed it. The pretend horror was laughable compared to what they had experienced with sopaths.

Thereafter Clark and Dreda associated more closely with Nefer, so that they seemed almost like three siblings. They were getting used to each other despite their formidable difference. The rest of the fair went well.

"Thank you," Nefer said politely as they went home. "That was fun."

"We can drop you off at your house," Bunty said.

"No thank you, Mister Slate. My folks think I spent the day at the children's library." They had to laugh.

They got out at home, and Nefer promptly disappeared.

"She's sweet on daddy, all right," Dreda said without jealously.

"She's a sopath!" Clark protested. "I touched her and felt that emptiness."

"So did I. They get crushes too."

"That could explain why she was so well behaved," Bunty said. "She wants you to like her, Abner."

"She wants me to have sex with her!"

"That, too," Bunty agreed. "Be careful of her, Abner. Don't rebuff her in such a way as to make her feel like a woman scorned."

Because any sopath was dangerous, and this one doubly so. "She is quite explicit about what she wants of me. There's no way I can oblige it. You know that."

"Keep telling her no," Dreda said. "But leave a little bit of doubt in your voice, so she thinks maybe you don't really mean it. Like mommy when she says she'll spank us if we don't behave."

"I never spanked you!" Bunty protested indignantly.

"But you threatened to. That's what I mean."

"Even when we did misbehave," Clark said.

Bunty lifted her hands in surrender. "Point made."

"But that's tacitly encouraging her!" Abner said.

"It's the safest course, dear. Her interest in you is a lever that can make her emulate a conscience. Nothing else will."

And that was excellent advice. "But with luck I'll never see her again."

"She'll be back," Dreda said. "She wants to get close to you."

She was surely correct, again.

CHAPTER 5

For a while things were relatively calm. The traps continued to get sopaths, and the detention cellar continued to take them out. Most were young, three or four years old, and inexperienced, easy prey. It was the older ones, like Nefer, that were dangerous, because they were learning to emulate normals, and some were quite good at it.

"We're losing ground," Sylvia said. "We're taking out the less dangerous ones and missing the smart ones. We need a better way." All of them had become hardened to the necessity of killing children, or arranging for them to kill each other. It was an ugly business, but the alternative was uglier.

"We need to bring down the population so that sopaths aren't born anymore," Abner said.

She grimaced. "Lots of luck with that."

"There's the problem," he agreed. "Despite the increasing evidence, powerful political and religious groups still oppose any birth control, which is the only painless and effective way to do it. Families insist on their right to reproduce in any quantity they choose, and the least responsible ones increase their numbers disproportionately. So the global population continues to increase, and the ratio of sopaths increases." It was foolhardy but seemed to be an insoluble problem.

"We're limited to what we can do locally," Sylvia said. "Speaking of which, we have reports that a criminal has moved into the neighborhood, giving out guns and drugs to sopaths, making them twice as dangerous. We have to stop that."

"We do," he agreed. "Most sopaths have been armed only with knives. If they all get guns, we'll be in trouble."

"Serious trouble," she agreed. "That's why I'm going to make a formal complaint to the police."

"I'm not sure that's wise. Scuttlebutt is that some of them have connections with sopath girls."

"I've heard. Six-year-old prostitutes. In fact the criminal is a pedophile, trading his wares for sex. All the more reason to take him out."

"I'm not easy about this," Abner said.

"Because one of them told you not to trust the police? What other recourse do we have?"

"We could take him out ourselves."

She shook her head. "He's a normal. Criminal, but he has a soul. We kill sopaths, not normals, no matter how corrupt the normals may be."

"Maybe we should make an exception."

But she wouldn't have it. "I'm not crossing that line. I'll try the police, and hope for the best. If they don't act, then we can consider other ways to drive him out."

"I hope they act," Abner said. Maybe she was right.

Sylvia went to the police to make her case that day.

That evening when she stepped out of her house, a sopath shot her at point blank range, killing her, and fled before any neighbor could react.

It seemed they had the criminal's response. It was an open assassination, eliminating the one who wanted the criminal out of the neighborhood. A warning to others.

"The criminal must be paying off the police," Abner muttered to Bunty.

"I don't think so. They could have notified the man of the complaint and asked him to move out. Instead he killed the opposition."

That did seem more likely. The police might not be very effective, but they had tacitly cooperated with Pariah to deal with the sopaths. "But it was Sylvia's complaint that did her in."

"She tried to follow protocol," Bunty said. "Nefer's warning was on target: don't trust the police. Not because they're corrupt, but because there are times when standard practice, such as forwarding a complaint, doesn't work."

They held an emergency Pariah meeting. "We can't allow Sylvia's work to be destroyed," Abner said. "To do so would be to let the sopaths and their corrupt enablers win."

They were grief-stricken and angry about the assassination, but confused. "What can we do, if the police can't help us?" a man asked.

"We can take out the criminal directly," Abner said. "That would eliminate the present problem and serve as a warning to those who try to arm the sopaths."

"How?"

"I believe I have a connection. The less said about it the better."

They agreed to let him try it his way. They did not inquire about the details.

Abner discussed it with his family. "I have two serious reservations. First, do we really want to get into the business of killing people with souls? That pedophile may be a wretch, but he surely has a soul."

"He's acting like a sopath," Bunty said. "I'm willing to classify him as a fellow traveler, to be treated much the same. In fact I would rather kill a criminal souler, than a civilized sopath."

Abner looked at the children. They nodded, taking their cue from Bunty. "But how?" Clark asked.

"I'm thinking of Nefer," Abner said. "But I'm wary of her price. That's my second reservation."

"We can talk with her," Bunty said with resignation.

Abner called Nefer's cell phone, let it ring once, and disconnected. That was the signal.

In five minutes she was there. "You want me!"

"We have a job for you," Abner said grimly. "We need to talk terms."

"That child fucker," she said wisely.

"The pedophile. You were right about the police," Abner said. "Sylvia of Pariah went to them to ask that they arrest the man. Instead they gave the criminal a warning, and he sent a sopath to kill her."

She nodded. "The bad guys play hardball."

"We can play hardball too. You could take him out."

She didn't blanch. "Sure. What's your offer?"

Abner braced himself. "What do you want?"

"A night in bed with you, naked, and you let me do anything I want."

Clark and Dreda smiled, having seen that coming. Bunty's face remained studiedly neutral.

"No." But he remembered to say the word without special force. "What else will you trade for?"

"You wouldn't have to do anything," Nefer said. "You could just lie there. Just ignore me."

As if she'd ever let him do that! "What else?" Abner repeated.

Nefer tried yet again. "When I kiss you, firm your lips a little. And when I put it in me, you just let it spout. Nothing else."

He suppressed a violent negation. "That was not what I meant." As she surely understood.

"What else?" Bunty inquired with tight control. She could afford to play the part of a jealous female.

The girl sighed. "A get out of jail free card."

"A what?"

"The police catch me, I call you and you come bail me out, no questions."

"Why would they let me do that?"

"They'll think I'm your sopath mistress. Grist for the dossier. Blackmail ammunition. They'll like that."

"It would ruin my reputation!"

She nodded. "Maybe I'll get killed first. Then you won't have to pay."

"But if it happens--"

"So maybe easier to have me in bed. I won't tell."

"My wife would be outraged."

"Maybe not," Nefer said. "She knows it's just a deal, like buying a car." As a sopath, she was not concerned with family loyalty.

Abner looked desperately at Bunty. Bunty looked at Nefer. "This would be a single night? No repeats?"

The girl hesitated, then agreed. "One shot. For this one deal. Other deals, other bargains."

"Suppose I was there watching?"

Another hesitation. "If you didn't interfere." As a sopath she didn't care about Bunty's sentiments, just whether she would act to stop it.

"Before or after the assassination?"

"You're pretty cunning," Nefer said. "Okay, after. He's normal; he'll honor it."

"I can't say it appeals," Bunty said. "But it's a fair offer."

She was giving the sopath hope! Now he understood Bunty's strategy. Nefer would have no reason to be mad at her. Such anger could have deadly consequences. "No. I'll make the get out of jail deal."

"Suit yourself. Maybe next time we can fuck." Nefer, disappointed, slipped out.

"She's really, really sweet on you, daddy," Dreda said.

"And she's sort of pretty," Clark said.

"And that's enough of that," Bunty said severely.

The children laughed. They had been teasing her.

An hour later Abner's cell phone rang. It was Nefer. "I made the deal," she whispered. "Three fucks for a small gun. He's fetching the gun now. I'm naked in the back shed. I'll hide the phone in my pile of clothes and leave it on."

"Nefer, I can't go there to rescue you!" Abner protested.

"I know, Mr. Slate. I just want you with me like this, so if it goes wrong you'll know I really tried."

What could he do? "I'll listen."

"Great. Here he comes. Bye." There was a sound as she hid the phone.

"Here's the gun," a gruff man's voice said. "You'll get it after the third fuck tonight."

"I know," Nefer said. "Here's my split. Remember, put it in slowly."

"The hell." There was the sound of him getting down on her.

"Not so fast! It hurts!"

He answered only with an urgent grunt.

Nefer screamed. But Abner knew her well enough to recognize it as a performance rather than real pain. She was acting like a halfway novice girl, rather than an experienced whore. If the man had a small penis, she might not be hurting at all, but she wanted him to think he was really forcing her.

Then he spoke again. "What's that in your clothing?"

"My cell phone." The scuffle must have exposed it.

"Let's make sure it's off, you little bitch." Suddenly the connection broke.

Abner was left holding his phone, afraid to imagine what was happening. One thing was clear: Nefer really was doing it.

All he could do was wait, hoping for the best of this ugly transaction. It was hard to decide which was worse: what the girl was doing, or the way he had set her up for it. He certainly shared her guilt. He had knowingly sent a child to indulge in sex and murder.

Abner informed Bunty, who nodded. "We made a deal with the devil. But I hope she wins."

That night there was a knock on their back door. It was Nefer. There was blood all over her dress. She saw him, smiled, and collapsed.

Abner picked her up and carried her inside. "She's hurt," he announced.

"Put her in my bed," Dreda said. She kept her things in her room, but spent the nights sharing with Clark so as not to be alone. "It's a sopath room." Because Olive the sopath had used that room before her.

Bunty fetched a rubber sheet and laid it over the bed. Abner set the girl down. Nefer seemed to have lost consciousness;

it wasn't an act. Bunty examined the girl, then removed her clothing. "Stab wound, in the left forearm," she said. "She's lost blood."

"Her dress is soaked," Abner said.

"Not all of it is hers. Still, it's bad enough." She washed the arm, bandaged and bound it. Then she washed the rest of the girl's body. "She had sex." She cleaned that up too.

"They were into it when the phone connection cut off. Let's hope she got him."

"She must have. Obviously she managed to get close enough to use the knife."

"She knew how," he agreed, wondering how Nefer had managed to conceal the knife. Wouldn't the pedophile have checked for that as well as for the phone?

"She'll have to be watched tonight," Bunty said. "She might run a fever, and there could be damage that doesn't show, like a concussion. We'll have to be ready to take her to the hospital if she goes into shock." She fetched a nightie and worked it on to the girl's body.

They took turns watching. Nefer slept fitfully but seemed to be all right. Around midnight, on Abner's watch, she opened her eyes. "I got him."

"And he got you," Abner said.

"I had to wait until he got his cock--" she broke off, then corrected herself. "His penis into me before I stabbed him, when he was spouting. Then I did it."

"That was the way," Abner agreed, suppressing a wince. She was trying to honor the rules of the house about the vocabulary, but the reality remained ugly. "When he was distracted."

"Yes. It had to be then, because he was alert the rest of the time. He's done sopaths before. He fucks us, he doesn't trust us. He knew to turn off the phone. He grabbed my knife before he died. Twisted it from my hand. Stabbed me. Then he dropped. I had to get out from under him. Couldn't go home this way. Couldn't explain. Mom would never understand. Had to hide until dark. Came here."

"Yes. And I trust you also understand the other rules of the house. Harm any member of it and I will kill you regardless of any other deals." He knew he had to make a threat she understood.

"I know, Mr. Slate. I'm on normal behavior here. I need you." By normal she meant souled. She had no conscience, but she did understand civilized rules. And she did need the family, as people who could be trusted to help her and not to betray her. As long as she behaved.

"Good. We will take care of you." He was relieved.

She gazed at him, evidently in pain. "I did it for you, Mister Slate. Please. One kiss?"

"Do it," Bunty murmured behind him. "She earned it."

Indeed she had. This much he could do. He went to the bed, leaned down, and kissed Nefer on the mouth, the way he knew she wanted. She met him with surprising passion. She smiled blissfully, sighed, and sank back into unconsciousness.

He watched her as she slept. She looked angelic. What irony! Yet she had one curious quality: she wanted his favor. He had not understood before getting to know her that a sopath could have such a desire. It was a revelation. It meant that the desire for approval was independent of conscience.

Nefer woke when Dreda came to relieve Abner. "You want to talk," Nefer said to her.

"I'm not supposed to mess with you, just make sure you're okay," Dreda said uneasily.

"Talk about what?"

"Tell her," Abner murmured, delaying his departure. He had half a notion what was bothering Dreda.

"My brother was a sopath," Dreda said. "He tried to—to—"

"To fuck you," Nefer said. "I mean, rape you."

"Yes. He said he liked me, and he tried to do it, and I killed him." She gulped, and continued. "You like daddy. So sopaths can like people. Maybe I shouldn't have killed him."

"He lied. If he really liked you, he wouldn't have forced

you," Nefer said dismissively. "He just wanted the fuck. I mean, the sex. Some boys do. Even some girls. It can be fun." She sank back into sleep.

And there it was, confirmed, directly from a sopath. Nefer had said the same thing that Abner and Bunty had told Dreda at the outset. Abner could see that Dreda was immensely relieved. She had truly killed in self-defense.

And maybe he owed Nefer one, apart from the deal to kill the pedophile. Had she reassured Dreda because she wanted to please him? That seemed likely.

Later in the night Bunty rejoined him in bed. "Interesting sequence as Clark relieved me on watch," she said. "He was nervous, and Nefer asked him what he wanted. She's one sharp observer of people. He was mighty interested just where the man had put what. 'He put his hard penis in there,' she told him, showing her vagina and pointing. 'It hurt, some. Then I stabbed him to death. The way Dreda did with her brother.' That evidently satisfied Clark's guilty curiosity."

"From the horse's mouth, again," Abner said.

"She's a sopath, but there are things to appreciate about her."

"She's trying to ingratiate herself with our family."

"And succeeding," Bunty said. "I don't like any of this business, but we do need her for our dirty work."

"We do need her," he agreed morosely.

"You won't have to have sex with her, Abner. She's a sopath; the only way she knows to get the real appreciation of a man is sexual. That's immediate and powerful. If you could persuade her that you liked or respected her in some other manner, I think she'd be satisfied."

"What other manner?"

"I don't know. I think we need to study her. We are already learning things we never discovered with our own sopaths. Maybe if we understood their positive qualities as well as their negative ones, we'd be better able to deal with them."

"You are remarkably tolerant."

"Just practical. We need to handle the sopath challenge,

and ignorance won't help."

"You are surely right. You're more objective than I am. I love you."

She looked at him archly. "Are you just trying to get into my pants?"

He realized with surprise that he was turned on. "That too."

"Then take it all," she said, clasping him.

*

The item was in the morning newspaper. A criminal drug dealer, a known pedophile, had been stabbed to death by a person unknown. The conjecture was that one of his victims had done it. It was scant on detail, probably deliberately, so as to keep the likely sopath aspect out of the news.

The counter-message had been delivered: the criminal element would not be tolerated in this neighborhood. That assassination would be met by assassination. It was hardball. Would that be effective? Abner was gambling his reputation with Pariah that it would be, but only time would tell.

Meanwhile they had Nefer as a patient. She seemed somewhat recovered, but not ready to leave on her own power. She wasn't faking it; she really was weak from blood loss. "Your family will be concerned," Bunty told her as she fed her some breakfast.

Nefer was surprised. "I guess so." She was a sopath; she lacked empathy. Her concern of the night had been only to conceal her state from those who would not understand, complicating her life.

"Can you call them?"

"Sure." Nefer found her cell phone and touched the number. "Mom? I had an accident and couldn't make it home last night." She paused. "Yes, I sneaked out. I'm sorry." Another pause. "I'm at a friend's house. It's okay." Another pause. Then she covered the mouthpiece. "She wants to know where. You'll have to tell her. Name's Johna Biggs." She handed the phone to Bunty.

Bunty picked right up on it. "Mrs. Biggs? I'm Bunty Slate. It seems Nefer came over to see my daughter, but was intercepted by a sopath. She got away, but was stabbed in the arm. We had to take her in. She was unconscious much of the night, but seems to be recovering now. Yes, of course. Here is our address." She concluded the call and returned the phone to Nefer.

"You're a good liar," the girl said admiringly.

"It was as close to the truth as she needs to know. She's on her way here." Bunty quirked a smile. "Does this count as fulfilling a get out of jail card?"

"No," Abner said. "She got injured in the course of doing our dirty job. We still owe her the bail."

"And you kissed me," Nefer said. Then she closed her eyes and sank back into sleep.

"She's right," Abner said to Bunty. "You *are* a good liar."

"We do what we have to do. All of our lives would be in jeopardy if word of her part in the assassination got out."

"Remember," Bunty cautioned the children. "Her folks don't know she's a sopath. You are now officially Nefer's little friends."

"Got it," Dreda agreed.

"I can lie too." Clark nodded in agreement.

Mrs. Biggs arrived, the woman Abner had seen in the store. She hurried to the girl. "My baby! We were so worried!"

"I was a bad girl," Nefer confessed. "I snuck out and got in bad trouble." Then she started crying.

Her mother was immediately comforting. It was clear that Nefer knew how to manage her.

In due course Nefer was packed into her mother's car and taken home. The family could finally relax.

"But you know, we have crossed the line," Bunty said. "We knowingly used a sopath to kill a normal."

Exactly. "We do what we have to do. We are at war."

And, indeed, so it seemed.

The Pariahs were on full alert for the next few days, but the neighborhood was quiet. Either their watchfulness was effective, or the criminals had not yet tried to strike back. Unless the message had been received, and there would be no further trouble.

Then a bomb exploded, sending a car careening out of control. They studied the site, and concluded that it was a mine that had been buried under a loose section of the pavement, primed to detonate when a car tire pressed it flat.

The war was not over.

"Metal detectors," Abner said. "We need to spot any more of those things that show up."

They got the detectors, but two more cars were wrecked before they zeroed in on an unexploded mine. One of the Pariahs knew how to handle it. They deactivated it, dug it up, and stored it in a safe place.

There was a memorial service for Sylvia, attended by more than just Pariahs. She had been a force for good in the neighborhood. Even several policemen attended, and some spoke. It was evident that they were sorry about what happened.

The police chief approached Abner after the service. "Someone will have to take her place," he said. "You could do it."

"Me! I'm a family man."

"Who takes out sopaths. Who doesn't like criminals. Or so I hear. Well, what you do is your own business. But watch your back. That pedo was part of a larger operation, and they don't like to be challenged. They use the sopaths as drug runners. Some of them can be bought for just candy. We can't be everywhere all the time, and now we know how they react to a straightforward complaint. So we won't try that again. But we'll support you in our fashion."

"Thank you," Abner said tightly.

There seemed to be no alternative. He met with the Pariah members and informally assumed the mantle of their local leader. This meant that newly bereaved sopath survivors would be directed to him, and he would have to try to find assistance for them. It promised to be a headache, but someone had to do it.

They continued to take out sopaths, mostly young ones,

ages three and four, who managed to get out but had not yet become wary of candy. It was evident that this was a rising global problem; their neighborhood was typical, not special.

The older sopaths, ages five, six, and seven, were fewer in number, but canny and dangerous. They carried drugs and guns, delivering to that broad market for both. And child prostitution.

Abner took Dreda to visit Nefer at her home, during her recovery. She was confined to her room for health reasons, and was antsy. Her arm was healing without complications. Dreda made a show of hugging her, and Nefer hugged her back. Then Abner talked with Mrs. Biggs while the two children chatted by themselves. After half an hour Abner went to fetch Dreda.

"I have cookies," Mrs. Biggs said. "This way."

"I'm tired of cookies," Nefer said. So Dreda went with the woman, leaving Abner alone with Nefer for the moment.

"I gave Dreda the scoop," Nefer said. "Please."

He knew what she wanted. He sat down beside her, put his hands on her shoulders, and kissed her on the mouth. Again he felt her surprisingly mature passion.

"Thanks," she breathed.

Nefer was, bit by bit, having her way with him.

On the way home, Dreda filled him in. "She did sneak out some. She knows some normal children she gets information from. She trades feels for it with the boys, stolen trinkets with the girls. She gave me the local address of the criminal sin—syndi—"

"Syndicate."

"Syndicate, where they distribute the drugs."

"That's what we need to know," Abner said. "Thank you, Dreda. I know you don't like being friendly with a sopath, but it really helps."

"Actually, she's not bad, now that she's treating me like a friend. It's an act, but it works. You're the one she wants."

"I kissed her. I can do that much."

"She'd do anything for a kiss, and more if you let her touch you where she wants. Maybe you should let yourself like her a little, daddy."

"I'll try," he said.

There were Pariahs who knew how to use the Internet to track things down. They verified that the local source of the drugs was the address Nefer had given. They focused on it, intercepting more of the older sopaths now that they knew where to find them.

Then as Abner was backing out of his carport, there was an explosion under his car. The car was heaved up and thrown on its side. Only the secure seat belt saved him from a severe battering or worse. As it was, he was knocked out for a moment. He came to as Bunty was struggling to get him freed from the harness and out of the burning car.

The syndicate had zeroed in on him and tried to assassinate him, just as it had Sylvia.

"They're playing for keeps!" Bunty said as she got him into the house and into bed. "Abner, we can't continue like this!"

"We can't quit, either," he said. "We can't turn the neighborhood over to the criminals and sopaths."

She shook her head, knowing he was right.

He spent three days recovering, on Bunty's insistence. He was bruised all over, and had an oppressive headache, but nothing was broken. Pariahs visited, commiserating.

So did Nefer. "Don't tell me you care," he teased her weakly.

"I do care," she said. "You still owe me a jailbreak."

Oh, of course. Trust her to have a selfishly practical motive. "I will honor it, if the time comes."

"Do you want me to get in bed with you and rev you up?"

Was she trying to be helpful? "Thanks, no. Why did you come?"

"You're going to get them back, right? Same way as we took out that pedo?"

He hadn't thought of that. "I don't think the same ploy will work this time. They aren't pedophiles."

"You've got that bomb."

"Return the favor? Suddenly I like the way your mind works, Nefer. But I fear planting it where it counts would be impossible to accomplish. They'll have guard dogs and electronic sensors."

"But a sopath runner could get in. Maybe plant the bomb."

"That thing must weigh a hundred pounds."

"I could tote it on a wagon. Set it off in the house."

"It would be suicide!"

"But it would get them."

He stared at her. "Are you serious? You're a sopath, you care for your own hide above all else."

"I'd do it for you."

"No."

"Take me in bed with you now, and I'll do it tonight."

"You're crazy!"

"No. But maybe in love."

"You're a child and a sopath. How can you love anyone other than yourself?"

"I'm a child and a sopath," she agreed. "But I think I love you. Just being near you turns me on."

Abner considered that. "May I consult with my wife?"

"Consult with them all. It's a deal I'll make."

In moments the family was there with them. "Nefer has offered to be a suicide bomber, to take out the criminal distribution center. In return for sex with me. She says she loves me. Is this possible?"

The three of them focused on Nefer. "Let me hold your hand a moment," Bunty told her.

Nefer offered it. Bunty took it and put her finger on the wrist, checking the pulse. "Now take her other hand, Abner."

What was Bunty up to? Abner reached and took the girl's other hand.

"Suddenly her pulse is accelerating," Bunty said. "Now kiss her."

Abner brought the girl to him and kissed her gently on the mouth.

"Racing," Bunty announced as she released Nefer's hand. "She either loves you or hates you."

"I love him," Nefer said. "I want to make him love me back, or at least like me a little. Knowing I'm a sopath."

Bunty nodded. "As a sopath, she lacks civilized limits. A normal child would suppress romantic or sexual appetite for an adult, feeling shame. Nefer has no such restraint. She loves you and is bargaining openly for your return love. It's a fair offer."

"The hell it is!" he snapped. "I would not take advantage of her like that, either way."

"I know you wouldn't, dear. My point is that she is willing to do anything to win your favor, including suicide. That has to be respected."

"You're helping me!" Nefer said, amazed.

"I'm helping the man I love to accomplish his purpose. There are nuances that you are not equipped to understand, Nefer, but the essence is that yes, I support your case."

Taken aback, Abner looked at Clark and Dreda. "What's your take on this?"

"When she's acting decent, she's not bad," Clark said.

"I don't want her to die," Dreda said. "I like her." That was a formidable admission.

Now Nefer spoke. "You know I'm only pretending. I'm not your friend, Dreda. I can't be anybody's friend."

Dreda looked cannily at her. "Daddy loves me. You love daddy."

"So?"

"Let me interpret," Bunty said. "A significant part of what Abner is, is his love for his family. We're not his original family, but we've all had similar experiences with sopaths and we understand him, and he understands us. We fulfill each other. We all hate sopaths. But now we are coming to accept you, despite your nature, in part because you love Abner too. Maybe in a different way, but you do. You are coming to accept us because you can't love Abner without loving what he loves too."

"Sure I can. I don't care who else he loves."

"And you're not jealous of his love for Clark and Dreda?"

"They don't want to have sex with him."

"Point taken," Bunty said. "But what about me? I do want to have sex with him."

Nefer gazed thoughtfully at her. "And you're helping me. I don't understand that."

"Maybe I think that if he had sex with you, then the challenge would be gone and you'd lose interest and go away."

"Bunty!" Abner protested.

Nefer shook her head. "Wouldn't work. I'd want him to keep fucking and fucking me all the time."

"I'm not going to do that!" Abner said.

"I know," Nefer said. "But at least this way I can be close to you."

"You can be close to him by being close to Clark and Dreda," Bunty said. "If he knows you'll be protecting them from harm, he'll value you more."

The girl pondered, working it out. "That's right. He'd kill me if I did anything bad to you or them, but if I help them, maybe he'll like me."

Abner saw his opportunity. "Maybe I will," he agreed.

"Via that avenue you can be Dreda's friend," Bunty said. "Perhaps not one to be completely trusted, but there are different types of friends."

Nefer stood there, mulling it over. Then tears started rolling down her face. "I—can—be. A friend."

Dreda put her arms around Nefer. Then the others closed in, and they were a close group with Nefer in the center. It was similar to their nightly grief sessions, but this was a kind of joy.

After a moment they separated. "Here is another truth," Bunty said to Nefer. "When you pretend long enough, you can come to accept it as a kind of reality. To be what you pretend to be. You will never have a conscience or feel remorse, but as long as you act as if you do, you can have the benefits they bring. Including survival."

"I pretend at home," Nefer said. "But they don't know."

"We *do* know," Abner said. The girl was a consummate little actress emulating normal feelings she lacked, but was committed in her fashion. "That's the difference."

Nefer was still working it out. "So I don't have to fu—to have sex with you to make you like me. I just have to act like a normal."

"That's it," Abner agreed. "Now I can say it: I do like you, Nefer. Some. Maybe the way I might like a vicious guard dog, but as long as I know it is loyal to me, I like it."

She shook her head, bemused. "Weird."

The others laughed.

CHAPTER 6

"Understand," Abner said grimly. "We're not doing this because we like violence or killing, but because the criminals are trying to kill us and we have to be rid of them. We want them to conclude that this section of town is simply too dangerous for them to operate freely, so they will go elsewhere and leave us alone."

"We know, daddy," Dreda said. "It's like killing sopaths."

"Exactly. We are using Nefer because she can best do the job, not because we prefer her to you."

"We know," Clark said. "She doesn't mind killing."

"This is dangerous. We could both get killed. If so--"

"We know," Bunty said. "If you die, I will look for another man in Pariah, to maintain the family." She paused, then added "But please don't die."

"I'll certainly try. I love you."

Bunty paused again, opened her mouth, then dissolved into tears. They all clustered together, sharing another grief session, only this one was for him. In case he died. Bunty had tried to pass the prospect off incidentally, but gotten overwhelmed. They had all experienced the awful loss of their families, and didn't want it to happen again. And the fact was they did love each other, and the children. Their assembly as a *de facto* family might have been haphazard, but it had become quite real emotionally and practically.

Then Bunty was kissing him passionately. The children departed, letting her savagely seduce him. They understood.

That night he went out alone, fetched the wagon with the mine, and quietly wheeled it along the dark street. The heavy load was covered by a tarpaulin; it could have been anything from potatoes to children. They had considered a fancier camouflage, but concluded that it was pointless; the gangsters would quickly check it regardless. This needed to be brutally fast. He did not head directly to his destination, and checked everything around him to be sure no one was watching.

Nefer appeared, stepping from the shadow. "I have it, Mr. Slate."

"Not yet. It's heavy."

"Haul it to the low hill beyond the site. Then I'll ride it down."

"Nefer, it's a bomb!"

"It won't go off until I pull the plug." That was her way of describing the catch mechanism they had used to secure the mine. It was armed, but stifled; removal of that catch would set it off.

He did not argue further. He hauled the wagon along, and she paced him, peering around to be sure they were alone. He was highly conscious of the bomb, because they had packed it with kerosene-soaked wood chips and newspaper, hoping that it would set a fire when it went off. They did not want it going off prematurely.

In due course they were on the hill. A slight slope led down to the gangster's center of operations. "My turn," Nefer said, putting her hand on his on the handle.

"Remember, when you activate it, you will have perhaps ten seconds to get well away before it detonates," he reminded her. "It doesn't have a proper timing mechanism. Do it and run."

"I got it, Mr. Slate. Kiss me."

It was part of her price. He squatted before her, put his hands on her shoulders, and kissed her on the mouth. She pressed her lips into his, savoring it. She was good at kissing. She was behaving, but he knew she still wanted to seduce him if she could.

He broke the kiss and released her. "I love you," she said.

Then she lifted the handle, faced the target house and started walking. She had no trouble hauling the wagon behind her, because of the slope.

Abner moved behind a tree and watched. His heart was pounding from the danger and perhaps something else. It was all up to Nefer now, as it had been with the pedophile.

She proceeded resolutely down the street. When she approached the house, a man intercepted her. Abner could hear his challenge in the quiet night. "Who are you?"

"I'm a sopath," Nefer replied boldly, continuing to move forward. "News is you need runners. I brought my wagon, so I can carry a full load. Just give me the stuff and the addresses and the money."

The man paced her. "Not so fast, little so-bitch. What's under that tarp?"

"Its just a box for holding the stuff. I don't want to lose any. Where's the stash?"

But he was suspicious. "What's there? It stinks of kerosene."

She accelerated her pace, drawing close to the house. "Well so do you, creep."

"Hey, we got a smartass!" the man called.

Immediately several other men emerged from the house, surrounding them. One of them ripped the tarpaulin off, exposing the wooden box with its packing. The kerosene odor intensified. Abner could almost smell it from his distant vantage. In another moment they would discern the nature of this package.

Nefer reached inside and yanked off the protective tie, activating the bomb. She bolted away.

"Grab her!" the first man cried, apparently not catching on to the danger they were in.

The man closest to Nefer reached out to snag her as she passed him. She brought her head down and bit his hand.

"Yow!" he bellowed, grabbing for her again. He caught her and hauled her into him.

The bomb detonated. It was a splendid explosion. The blast hurled the men outward, set their clothing on fire, and ignited the overhanging roof of the house. The man holding Nefer seemed to leap through the air, carrying her with him. His body was inadvertently shielding her from both the blast and the flames.

Then they fell, and both lay still as the fire spread across the house.

Abner was running toward them before he knew it. He saw Nefer's slight body pinned under that of the man. He hauled the man off her, then picked her up and carried her away. No one tried to stop him; they were all unconscious or dazed.

He halted only when he was well clear of the burning house, panting with the effort. Nefer lay in his arms, inert. Was she alive or dead?

"Oh, Nefer!" he said. "I didn't mean for you to get caught like that! You were so brave! I'll never forgive myself if you die!"

She did not react. Then, chiding himself for his foolishness, he lifted her head to his face and kissed her with the passion of guilt and fear.

Now she responded, weakly. "You kissed me."

"I did," he agreed, relieved. This was the first time he had kissed her of his own volition. "You were unconscious."

"Like kissing the princess awake."

"Like that," he agreed. "Are you all right? Can you walk?"

"I don't know. I feel woozy and sort of bruised."

"You were too near the explosion. That man landed on you, although his body shielded you from the flames. Oh, Nefer, I'm so glad you made it!"

"So am I." She looked sharply at him, her wooziness dissipating. "You could have left me there."

"They would have killed you!"

"Yes. Saved you some trouble. You know I still want to get you into my pants."

"And you know I won't do it."

Again that calculating look. "Are you sure, Mister Slate?"

He had to be painfully honest. "No. Call me Abner; I think you have earned it."

She was pleased. "Gee. Thanks, Abner." Then she got serious. "You could have been sure, if you'd let me die. It would have been easy."

"Not for me. I have a soul and a conscience. I couldn't let you die if I could prevent it."

"And maybe you want me, a little."

He was supposed to play her along, not cutting off her hope, so that she would continue to help him. Was that really all there was to it? "Maybe."

"And as you said, if you pretend long enough, you can maybe start being what you pretend to be."

She had him in a neat trap. There *was* a guilty twinge of desire. She had become more of a person to him, less of a sopath. She was playing him as he was playing her. "Maybe by the time I'm ready to let you seduce me, you'll have developed a conscience and won't do it." The subtext there was that she would never develop a conscience, and his capitulation was similarly unlikely.

"Maybe," she agreed, satisfied. She was still a child and some things escaped her. All she saw was the chance she might succeed. He was deceiving her in her expectation, not his actual words. That was perhaps a fair compromise.

Nefer remained weak and dizzy, so he carried her back to her home. "You'll tell your family something," he said. "You need several days of rest."

"I do. Kiss me again, Abner."

He kissed her, feeling her passion again, appalled at himself for the temptation to respond to it, and then let her fade into the shadow.

Abner returned home. "We took it out," he reported. "Nefer did it, really. I owe her, and she knows it. I'm letting her call me Abner. We're using each other, but I can't be sure who is winning."

"We do play a dangerous game, in more than one respect," Bunty said. "With luck this will finish our association with her."

"With luck," he agreed, not believing it. For one thing, he now owed her two get out of jail free cards.

Abner abruptly lost his job. Someone had sent his employer a note connecting him to a supposedly malign Pariah organization, and that was enough to promote a spot layoff. He could neither prevent the layoff nor prove the accusations were untrue. Paranoia was rampant, and he was just another casualty. The criminals had found another way to score.

"We can get by," Bunty said. "My job will sustain us." But they both knew that would only delay their bankruptcy.

"Pariah," Clark said. "They need recruiters."

Abner nodded. He put in an application.

News came down immediately from the national pariah office, as though they had anticipated his need. Maybe it was common among Pariah activists. They needed a traveling organizer, and he was a prime prospect. But there might be danger.

They hardly hesitated. Abner took the job. They decided to sell the house, buy a motor home, and travel as a family. That would get them out of their neighborhood while doing Pariah some good. Between the war with the criminals and his joblessness, this had become an awkward neighborhood to live in. It was summer, so school for the children was not a problem.

They got busy quietly organizing for the change of lifestyle. Abner discussed it with other Pariah members, arranging for another person to take over the local reins. They would not give up the campaign, but would be more cautious than Abner had been.

His caution was justified. Several days later Nefer appeared at his house. Bunty let her in the front door. She was coated in ashes and her hair was wild. "Mister Slate, I need your help."

Abner exchanged a fleeting glance with Bunty. That formal address was surely significant. "What is it?"

"The crooks must've recognized me. They fire-bombed my

house. I got my folks out, but I can't stay with them any more."

Clark and Dreda had joined them. "Why?" Clark asked.

"Because I'm dead."

"You mean they will kill you, now that they have identified you and failed the first time?" Bunty asked.

"No. It's complicated. Damn!" She looked confused, not able to speak coherently. It was getting to her.

Bunty looked meaningfully at Abner. He responded by going to Nefer, picking her up, then sitting in the easy chair, holding her close on his lap, her head against his chest. "Take your time," he told her.

She melted, much as a real girl would. Her lack of a conscience did not affect her need for comfort, and he was perhaps the only one who could provide it. Then she talked. "I was out scouting around. Crooks are like sopaths; you can't trust them. So I was alert. I heard something, so I sneaked around to watch without being seen. Someone was pouring water or something behind our house. It was a girl about my size. Then I saw a flash, and realized what it was: kerosene. They sent a sopath to firebomb my house, the same way as we firebombed theirs. It was another warning. They are striking back. They don't care if I live or die, they just want me to stop bothering them."

She paused, collecting her thoughts. Abner held her close and stroked her hair. He saw Dreda nod approvingly: he was pacifying the sopath. "True," he agreed. "But that was not the whole of it."

"It was too late to stop the fire," Nefer continued. "But not too late to act. I ran up behind her and stabbed her through the back. Then I heaved her into the fire. Then I ran around, went inside where it wasn't burning yet, and screamed to my folks to wake up, the house was burning. I really made a racket. I got them up and out. Then I told them: the firebombing was because of me, and they wouldn't be safe as long as I lived. So I had to be dead. I told them how I caught the girl who set the fire and threw her into it. She had to be me, burned to death, and they had to accept that. So they would be left alone. They looked at the fire and believed. I left them and came here. Mister Slate, I need you to get me out of here, somehow, where I'll never be recognized."

"Yes you do," Abner agreed.

"We can do it," Bunty said. "We are about to travel."

"I didn't mean you had to be with me," Nefer said. "I meant to put me in an orphanage or something where I'll be anonymous and safe. I can't do that myself, but maybe Pariah could."

"No local orphanage would take you," Bunty said. "You're a sopath. They'll be alert for that."

"Some other town, then, where they don't know about sopaths."

Clark and Dreda laughed. The whole world knew about sopaths by now. But they had to do something for her.

A look passed around the family. The children nodded. Bunty pursed her lips, but nodded also.

"We'll take you," Abner said. "We owe you."

"You owe me a get out of jail free card," Nefer said. "Only I want to be put *in* jail, to save my hide and leave my folks safe. I owe them that."

And the girl did honor the deals she made, not from conscience but because she had learned that it paid in the long term to do so. She had to make it safe for her family.

"That's a rational assessment," Bunty said. "But we're not entirely rational. We have consciences. You incurred this problem because you helped us fight the criminals. We'll take care of you."

"But you know I want to--" Nefer shrugged. "You know what I want." She gazed at Abner, letting her longing show. Her desire for him seemed to have intensified rather than faded. He reminded himself again that as a sopath she lacked natural restraints. She was a child, but it was naked lust she felt.

"We do," Bunty said. "But as I said, we are not entirely rational. We are prepared to take the risk, if you are prepared to behave like a family member. In fact, we can probably use you, because of your ability to identify other sopaths."

"I'd rather be with you," Nefer said. "But you don't owe me that. I'm trying to be fair. It's not easy for me."

"It's not easy for anyone," Bunty said. "We will guide you. You know the general rules."

"I do." Then, relieved, the girl relaxed. They were settling their debt to her the hard way.

It was in the newspaper next day: a house had burned down, the adults had escaped, but their daughter had burned to death. There would be a funeral for her.

Nefer was officially dead.

They kept her out of sight, but did not change her name. It was a nickname anyway, not her legal one. She cooperated perfectly, knowing that discovery was likely to mean her death. She slept in a nook in the cellar, her rat hole as she called it. She donned a blond wig that transformed her appearance, and very innocent childish clothing. She was probably unrecognizable, even to those who had known her reasonably well.

"We need to incorporate Nefer in such a way that no one will ever suspect her nature," Bunty said.

"You have something in mind?"

"She looks angelic. Maybe we could make her act angelic."

"I am not following you."

"We'll be traveling as a close-knit family. We could be religious. At least to the point of attending local church services. Participating in their events."

"I'm still not following."

"Singing in the choir, for example. We can sing average, but Nefer can sing well. She told me she sang in her family's choir."

"But sopaths don't give half a crap for religion."

"But they can fake it, when they want to."

Maybe it would help. "Let's ask her, and hear her sing."

"Nefer!" Bunty called.

The girl appeared almost immediately. "Whatever it is, I'll do it."

"We understand you can sing."

"Sure, when I have to. I was the best singer they had in the choir." Modesty was not a sopath trait.

"We're thinking of singing in local churches as we travel," Bunty said. "To seem more like a religious family. Will you join us?"

"You want me to?" Nefer asked Abner.

He was unwilling to let his leverage on her be the only reason. "Yes. But this is optional. Let me state my points."

"That's okay, Abner. I'll do it for you."

"First, it would help the Pariah culture effort, because not everyone can sing, and few can sing well. If you can sing well—well, a good lead singer can help the others stay on track, and make them seem better too."

"I know. I did it all the time."

"Second, it would help conceal your nature, because no one would think a sopath could sing a religious song."

"That's crazy! I don't care about religion, but I do like to sing, because it's a way to soften people up for whatever I want, and some of those hymns are really good for that."

Bunty smiled. "We soulers have some crazy notions."

Abner made a mental note: sopaths had no emotional appreciation for the arts, because those stemmed from symbolism and empathy. Nefer cynically used her talent to get things for herself, not for its own sake.

"Okay, let's see what we have here," Abner said. "See how we integrate."

They assembled the family. "We're about to see how well Nefer can sing," Abner told the children. "And whether she can help us to sing a hymn better." He looked at Nefer. "Is there one you prefer?"

"*Oh Holy Night*. It's got flow and power, and people get all mushy over that."

"Can you sing it a cappella?"

For answer, Nefer simply started singing. "Oh holy night, the stars are brightly shining. It is the night of our dear Saviour's birth." The others listened silently, surprised first that she clearly had no trouble with the tune, words, or religious theme, and second by the quality of her voice. She had not exaggerated; she was an excellent singer. Her tone was like a bell, and she had perfect pitch. It was a pleasure to listen to her. They were indeed getting mushy, as she put it.

Nefer continued through the whole hymn, hitting the high notes seemingly without effort, filling the room and the house with the power of her voice. "...oh night divine!"

Then she looked at Abner.

"You have a really beautiful singing voice," he said, awed. "It sends shivers down my spine."

"Okay," Nefer said. "I'll do it because I'll do anything to oblige you, Abner, and because you're right, it'll hide me so I won't get killed as a sopath. But mainly because the thought of sending shivers down your spine maybe all the way to your, your--"

"Manhood," Bunty supplied with a smile.

"Yeah. That sends shivers through *me*. Maybe I can evoke your passion with my voice." She was learning not to say "Get you to fuck me." Abner appreciated that.

"Maybe you can," he agreed, not insincerely.

That night he confessed his concern to Bunty. "That girl is too pretty, too clever, too talented. She is gaining on me. I fear where this is leading. I am revolted, but it's there."

"Don't be concerned."

"But Bunty, sometimes I even think I would *like* having sex with her. You mean everything to me, but she's so ardent, so persistent. I am no longer seeing her quite as a sopath, or a child. She's a cynical young woman."

"Get real, Abner," she said firmly. "We don't live in the 'nice' culture we once did. We have to do things that would have been unthinkable before. We lie, we use people like her, we kill children, we kill grown criminals with souls. The old morality is dead. If I thought your having sex with a more-than-willing rational child would enable us to solve the problem of sopaths, I'd put you in bed with her and not let you out until you satisfied her. I know the children would agree."

"You can't be serious!"

"I *am* serious. But I don't believe it would do the job, so it's academic. If she had sex with you once, she'd expect it again, and there would be no end to it. It remains her best expression of the love she feels for you." She smiled briefly. "I know exactly how that is. You have that magnetism springing from your soul, bending women to your will."

"That's really no credit on me."

"The credit is your discipline and conscience. You are not allowing your power to corrupt you."

"Thank you," he said, bemused.

"We can use her, we need her, and she's settling for little enough, considering her passion. Let's let it rest there."

"You frighten me almost as much as she does."

"We're women." Then she set about seducing him, which required very little effort. He might feel some temptation for touching the girl, but he had a full-blown passion for the woman, and she knew it and shared it.

There was a problem with the motor home they found on sale: it slept four, two adults and two children. They could not afford more, and more would have been suspicious. Space was tight; there simply was not room for another person.

It was Nefer who came up with the answer. "We hope this puts off the criminals, and that they're not after any of us anymore. But we can't be sure. Someone needs to be on watch all the time. We can take turns around the clock, and when it's my turn I swear I'll be as good a watch as you can find. When I sleep, it will be in whichever bed isn't being used by the one who is on watch. Or I'll sleep in the daytime, hiding."

"Something like that should work," Abner agreed. Her intelligence also attracted him, but he couldn't say that.

It took another two weeks to finally get things cleared and start moving. During that time they also practiced family singing, and Nefer continued to cooperate fully, enchanting them all with her beautiful voice. "She's trying to be a full member of the family," Bunty murmured during a tryst. "As she was with her original family. She's eerily good at it. I confess I'm coming to like her."

"She's a sopath," he reminded her.

"That's what makes it eerie. It's like having a tame rattle-snake in the house, uncaged."

It was, indeed.

They departed without ceremony, the Pariahs knowing only that Abner had become a traveling organizer who didn't want publicity because of the general prejudice against Pariahs.

The first night they parked in a park without connections, so it was little used despite being cheap. They were prepared with plenty of food and water. Bunty cooked a respectable dinner, they practiced singing a hymn, and they settled down for the night.

"I'll take first watch," Nefer said. "I'll prowl the neighborhood to make sure no one is sneaking up on us."

"Not just yet," Abner said. "First we'll have a family mission meeting. You can move around and peer out the windows, but you need to hear this."

"There's something we don't know?" Clark asked.

"There is," Bunty said. She knew the details, but had kept silent.

Then in darkness Abner informed the children of the rest of his mission. "The organization mission is a cover," he said. "I will do it, going to a list of towns across the country, meeting with local Pariah groups and showing them how to organize and establish relations with the national organization. It will do them good, because they will have information and support. But the real mission is to investigate two mysterious towns, Sweetpea and Sauerkraut."

They all laughed, thinking it a joke. Which made Abner think again. Nefer had laughed too, which meant that sopaths could appreciate humor. Which meant in turn that humor was not connected to the soul. He hadn't thought about it before.

Thinking it was funny when a fat man slipped on a banana peel and fell on his bottom required no empathy, no real feeling for the man, who might be hurt. Humor could be cruel, as when bullies joked at a victims' expense. Most humor was innocent, as this was, an oddity of names.

"No joke," Abner said. "Those really are the names. Sweetpea formed around a large diabetes treatment complex."

There was silence, so Bunty explained. "Diabetes is an illness affecting the metabolism of sugar. The body uses insulin to metabolize sugars, and diabetics either lack insulin or are unable to use it effectively. So sugar accumulates in the blood. To reduce it, the body gets extremely thirsty and produces a lot of urine, which can be quite sweet because of the sugar. The larger picture is more complicated than that, but that explains the name."

There was a pause as the children figured it out. "Pee!" Clark said. "They pee a lot!"

"And it's sweet from the sugar," Dreda said.

"Sweetpea," Nefer concluded. "It *is* a joke."

"In origin, yes," Abner agreed. "But diabetes can be lethally serious. Today, with more effective treatments, most sufferers get by tolerably well. Some take daily or hourly insulin shots, while some can get by on diet and exercise."

"Type One and Type Two," Clark said. "Now I remember. I had an uncle with it. He took shots."

"Most Type Ones need shots," Abner agreed. "Most Type Twos don't. The complex was for type ones. At any rate, that's in the past. In due course the complex moved elsewhere, and the town foundered economically but kept the name. Later a madman with a machine-gun mowed down half the remaining population before someone shot him to death. It was the worst tragedy to strike that part of the country. We don't know whether that history is relevant to the current phenomenon."

"Something's going on," Dreda said wisely. "A mystery."

"A mystery that relates to Pariah," Clark agreed.

"Yes," Abner agreed. "It is this: there are no sopaths there. None are born."

Now Nefer took note. "How can they be sure? Some sopaths are pretty good at hiding their nature. I'm one. I can always spot another sopath, but most soulers can't."

"Pariah has investigated," Abner said. "Quietly, of course. But they're sure. They think it was a sopath who gunned them down—he was just a child—but that's the last one reported. Pariah wants to know why. Did the massacre shock the survivors into taking action to stop it from ever happening again? If there's a secret to eliminating sopath births despite the shortage of souls, we really want to know it. That's part of my mission: to ascertain the reason, if I can. Without alerting others to my investigation."

"That's going to be tricky," Nefer said. "For one thing, how can you organize Pariahs if there are no sopaths? No sopaths means no sopath survivors. You have no connections."

"Exactly," Abner agreed, impressed again by her insight. "It's likely to be difficult. But I understand there are survivors there, who have moved in from elsewhere. I may have to pose as an amateur researcher writing a book, a history of odd towns, gathering all the obscure information I can. Hoping that somewhere in there is the answer."

"What about Sauerkraut?" Clark asked. "What's *its* history?"

"It was settled by a semi-religious outfit as a commune. They believed in being fruitful and multiplying, trying for ten or more children per mother. It was really a fertility cult, and the suspicion is that many of the children were fathered by the cult leader. Its population expanded rapidly and it was a thriving community. They evidently had plenty of money to support their population. Then the commune abruptly moved to a distant location, leaving their facilities to be sold off relatively cheaply. It was a mystery why. There were rumors of a curse on the premises. But bargain hunters soon moved in, obtaining nice residences at dirt-cheap prices. It became a viable town again."

"Where's the catch?" Dreda asked.

"It was that curse. There were a number of bad accidents, and some whole families got wiped out. Nothing they could pinpoint, just extremely bad luck. More folk moved in, but they too were soon dogged by mischief as the curse caught up with them. Before long there was a mass exodus. A number of families moved to neighboring Sweetpea. But others moved in, because of the bargain houses. So Sauerkraut is a violent place, in contrast to Sweetpea, with especially violent children."

"Sopaths!" Nefer exclaimed. "Sauerkraut has sopaths!"

"That would explain it," Abner agreed. "But why would sopaths be born there, and not at nearby Sweetpea? That's the current mystery."

"Sweetpea didn't share their secret," Clark suggested.

"But the two towns get along very well. Shipments from outside, such as fuel, food, and building materials, come to central warehouses in Sweetpea, which then shares them with Sauerkraut. Sauerkraut workers go to Sweetpea for employment. There's considerable economic and probably social exchange."

The children were thoughtful. "Sopaths in one town, none in the other, but they work together," Clark said. "That's funny."

"Not funny," Dreda said. "Odd."

"That's what I meant, twerp."

"Sweetpea has to know about the sopaths," Nefer said. "And maybe lets them work there, if they behave. They can behave if they have reason to." She herself being an example.

"But nobody wants more sopaths," Clark said. "Except maybe sopaths themselves."

"Sopaths don't want more sopaths either," Nefer said. "They can't be trusted."

"Not even you?" Dreda asked her.

"I don't want more sopaths," Nefer said. "They're nothing but trouble. And you know the only reason I'm behaving is because I want to stay close to Abner and maybe some day get him into my pants. You can't trust me to look out for anyone's interest but my own."

Clark looked at her. "What would you do if he did?"

Nefer paused thoughtfully. "If he fucked me? I mean, had sex with me?" She glanced quickly at Bunty. "Indulged me? I'd want him to do it again and again. I don't think I'd ever get enough of it."

Which was exactly what Bunty had said. Trust a woman to know the nature of such passion.

"So we could still trust you," Dreda said, neither surprised nor shocked. "Because you'd have to keep behaving to get him to keep doing you."

Nefer seemed surprised. "I guess so. I'm hooked. But I'm a rare case. Few sopaths ever get to know a souler well enough to fall in love, and few soulers would even give them the chance. You can't trust any *other* sopaths."

Abner and Bunty let the dialogue run its course. It actually was relevant to their mission, and it was confirming their prior judgment of Nefer's motives.

"And Sweetpea must know not to trust them," Clark said. "Unless there's something just as big to make them behave. Maybe not love, but something else."

"Fear," Nefer said. "We value our own hides."

"How could Sweetpea make them afraid?" Dreda asked.

"Beats me," Nefer said.

"They must have something," Abner said.

Dreda got a bright idea. "No sopaths in Sweetpea, because maybe they can wipe them out, and the sopaths know it, so they're afraid."

Nefer glanced at Abner. "*Are* they afraid?"

"There's no indication of that," Abner said. "It must be subtle, and sopaths aren't much for subtlety."

"The stupid ones aren't," Nefer said. "But smart ones can appreciate subtlety. I do. It's smart sopaths you have to be wary of."

"Yet the two towns get along well," Bunty said. "That doesn't seem like fear. More like respect."

"Sopaths respect only love and power," Nefer said. "Mostly power."

Clark struggled to work it out. "If sopaths don't want more sopaths born, and Sweetpea knows how to stop them, why doesn't Sweetpea share?"

"And why isn't Kraut mad if they don't?" Dreda asked.

Nefer spread her hands. "Beats me," she repeated.

The three looked at Abner. "So what's the answer?" Clark asked.

"That is what we are going there to find out," Abner said. "Because it could have global implications. I will need all of us to contribute to our effort. Someone may say something in the presence of a child, not thinking the child is listening or will understand."

"We'll do it," Dreda said confidently.

"Focus on two things," Bunty said. "Is there a way to stop sopaths being born? And is there a way to control sopaths without violence? We get along as a family, but as Nefer says, that's unlikely to work on the scale of two towns. We are surely not going into a paradise of love."

"What about sex?" Nefer asked. "We sopaths like sex and have no shame. Is Sweetpea a brothel?"

"Again, there is no evidence of that," Abner said. "They don't seem to have a red-light district."

"So there's something weird going on," Clark concluded. "We'll figure it out."

"A caution," Abner said. "There may be danger. The secret, whatever it may be, has been well kept. We have to appear as a naïve, innocent family. We don't want them to catch on that Nefer isn't a souler."

"I can play the part," Nefer said. "But I can tell a sopath when I see one. They'll probably have smart sopaths who will recognize me regardless."

"An alternative may be to let them believe that we don't know your nature, as your family didn't," Bunty said.

Nefer nodded. "That could work. Sopaths infiltrate regular families all the time. We aren't all destructive. Smart ones know they need the families."

"Then I think we are done," Abner said. "We can go about our family routine."

They did. Nefer kept watch, while the other children went to bed. Bunty and Abner went to bed too. They made quiet love, knowing Nefer was tuning in on it, but inured to it. Nefer seemed not to be jealous; she merely wanted to seduce Abner to have his ultimate attention, and to prove she could do it. She knew that any hostility to Bunty on her part would turn him off and get her in instant trouble.

Abner slept. They had agreed to one hour shifts for the children, two hours for the adults. That would carry them through a seven hour night.

He woke later to find Nefer settling down beside him, having taken Bunty's place in the shift change. Her bed was whichever one was unoccupied. She was unlikely to try anything, because Bunty was alert, being on watch, and because she knew Abner would reject it. But she did do one thing.

"Will you hold my hand, Abner?"

He smiled, took her hand, and returned to sleep. He hoped it would continue this easy, but suspected it would not.

Two hours later Bunty returned, having awakened Clark. The children had insisted on taking their turns rather than being coddled. Nefer went to take Clark's bed. "Thanks, Abner," she whispered as she departed.

"Welcome," he answered, bemused.

"She never slept," Bunty murmured. "She lay there thrilling to your touch. I believe she feels your soul, and that contact is like a drug, making her high."

"Damn, this is dangerous," he said. "As I said, I'm beginning to feel something for her."

"She knows it. That's what keeps her in line."

"But Bunty, this can't lead anywhere we want to go."

"Would you ever knowingly be seduced by a sopath, even if she was mature and breathtakingly lovely?"

"No!"

"Or a child?"

"No."

"Even one with a superlative singing voice?"

"No."

She was silent. She had made her case. His emotions might be tempted by Nefer, but his logic would always triumph. The real danger would be when Nefer herself came to that conclusion. In that sense his guilty slight temptation was an advantage, because she picked up on it, underestimating the formidable restraints, and continued her courtship. But it still bothered him.

In the morning they handled the early routine and got back on the highway. All of them were pleased: they had successfully navigated their first night on the road.

The children took turns sitting up front with Abner as he drove. The first was Dreda. "I never saw her so happy," she said. There was no need to clarify whom she meant. "She almost glowed in the dark."

"I held her hand while I slept," he said.

"I think she'd rather do that than get you into her pants, daddy."

And here he was discussing sex with his five-year-old daughter. But the world had changed, and she had learned about sex the hard way. "Why?"

"'Cause sex is over soon, but hands last."

Could that be true for the sopath? Nefer surely knew that if he had sex with her, he would lose interest in sex for several hours thereafter, as any man did. But they could hold hands continuously, even while he slept. For her, that might well be preferable. That would be marvelous. "That much I can give her."

CHAPTER 7

One of the perks of the position was constant contact with the national Pariah organization. Abner had a special cell phone that sent an automatic signal, tracking him. If that signal stopped, they would treat it as an emergency call and investigate immediately. He also used it to make ongoing reports, which he knew were recorded. Pariah wanted a complete record. No mysteries, secrets, or problems. Like the black box on airplanes, that record would help them fathom whatever might go wrong. When dealing with sopaths, as Pariah did, things were almost expected to go wrong.

"We have spent our first night on the road," he reported during a rest stop. "No problems."

The family and Nefer knew about the phone and record, but tuned them out. No one outside their family was supposed to know. If Abner was for any reason unable to carry the phone, one of the others would have to take it and make the reports. Even Nefer, ironically.

Their first stop was at a neighboring town that had a loose Pariah chapter but it wasn't well organized. Their members were vaguely stigmatized, they were having trouble coping with the constant influx of new survivors, and they were horrified by the prospect of encountering more sopaths.

"You need a leader who can establish relations with the local police," Abner said. "They will help you, if you learn to deal with sopaths."

"But we don't want any contact with sopaths!" their spokesman protested.

"By dealing with them I mean killing them," Abner said

bluntly. "You have already done it or you wouldn't be survivors. It is the only way to be rid of them."

"We just can't do that," the man said.

How well he understood. It was an expected answer. They had not had his military experience. His approach was intended as a kind of shock treatment. "Then avoid them as well as you can, and set up a school for survivors that has no sopaths in it. Set up a nondenominational church service too; you are apt to be excluded from conventional churches."

The spokesman nodded appreciatively. "That we can do." The man might have balked at the formidable task, but after appreciating the hell of killing children, he was glad to have an alternative.

"Another prospect is to form temporary families of survivors, so that the children are properly cared for and not discriminated against."

"Families?"

"My family was killed by my sopath child, until I killed her. Here is my Pariah wife Bunty: her family was similarly killed. We came together not from love but necessity: I needed a woman in the house and she needed economic support. Soon enough it became love, but for your purpose that is not necessary. We took in two sopath-orphaned children, Clark and Dreda, here, and we love them too. We do not deny or forget our original families, but now we are functioning as a composite family." He did not mention Nefer, who had remained to guard the motor home.

"From four real families?"

"Yes. Now we are a real family too. We never went through the paperwork of marriage or adoption, only a Pariah commitment, but we really are a family. You can do the same. It will be better for the children, and probably for the adults too. You all will have a common bond of understanding, as we do."

"A family," the man said. "But I may ask, what of, um--"

"We do make love," Bunty said. "That is part of the commitment. We fill the complete roles we have assumed."

"They sure do," Clark said. "It gets disgustingly mushy."

"And we have to go to our rooms," Dreda said.

The assembled members of the chapter exchanged glances, realizing the prospects. They could recover much of what they had lost, without having to struggle to relate to those who had never had the devastating experiences they had had. Without formally marrying or adopting. On an ad hoc basis, to get by in this time of loss and confusion.

"It doesn't have to be permanent," Abner said. "A temporary family will do." That would facilitate it, by allowing them to pool resources and take care of children without feeling that they were betraying their lost spouses or children. Functioning family units and a good, safe school would make this chapter far more viable, and the people far less miserable.

There were of course many details, and Bunty and the children helped relate to the women and children there. Everyone could see how much like a "real" family they seemed, and it didn't hurt that they freely showed love to each other. It was a viable alternative to the grief-stricken chaos these folk otherwise faced. The semblance of families would soon enough become practical reality, as they had discovered themselves. The common bond of sopath horror, and their need for mutual support, would solidify it rapidly.

In fact it occurred to Abner that this could be a prime reason he had been selected for the position. He and his new family were a living example of how well it could work. They were a model family, Pariah style.

They returned to the camper that evening. "Several people snooped around," Nefer reported. "But nobody tried to get inside."

That was just as well. They did not expect any suspicious behavior in the towns they visited, but had to remain alert. They would continue the watch roster at night. A Pariah organizer could be distrusted by outsiders.

"We seem to have had a successful contact," Bunty reported. "May it continue."

"So that no one will suspect the real mission," Nefer said.

"Exactly. We'll need to get you involved, to be sure no sopaths have infiltrated any of the chapters. The children say you can spot them more readily than they can."

"But I have to be hidden."

"Yes," Abner agreed. "But when we get well away from our home town, the chances of anyone knowing you will become remote. Your clothing, wig, and attitude further conceal you. I believe you can pose as a very shy friend of the children."

"Me, shy," she agreed, smiling. Shyness was a function of caring what others thought of a person, and sopaths didn't care, and weren't shy or reticent, as Nefer's references to wanting sex with him showed. Sopaths were unusually candid. Not because they had any reservations about lying, but because they didn't understand the concept of shocking others. They lied only to gain an advantage or protect themselves, never for social status.

In fact it occurred to him that Nefer was an ongoing lesson in the nature of the enemy, and as such was invaluable.

They kept Nefer out of sight while in the next two towns, but when they were far enough distant they had her substitute for Dreda, who kept watch behind. They were a family of four, and it was easy for Nefer to emulate the fourth. It seemed to work well enough. They helped set up a local church, and demonstrated a choir, and Nefer's evocative voice was persuasive.

"You're such a pretty child," a woman said appreciatively. "Do you really like your new family?"

"I adore them," Nefer replied shyly. "They really helped me after I lost my own family." Which was technically true, though she would readily have lied as persuasively as she needed to. So, for that matter, would have Clark and Dreda.

"You can make up similar temporary families," Abner reminded them. "If they don't work out, you can exchange members. Remember, every member of Pariah has had a similarly horrible experience, and will understand."

They wrapped up in good order, leaving behind another grateful Pariah chapter. When Abner called in to make his report, he was informed that prior chapters had spoken very well of him and his family. He was a success as an organizer.

"They're so naïve," Nefer remarked after her first such contact. "They don't question your family at all, really."

"And it is to safeguard us from similar unconscious naiveté that we have you along," Abner said. "If there are sopaths among them, we need to know, without alerting them that we know."

"I'll do anything you want, including that," she agreed, with a little flirt of her hip, a gesture she had picked up from Bunty. Abner reflected again how dangerously fascinating she would have been had she had an adult body.

As they traveled farther away, they started behaving more like a family of five, since no one knew of their origin. No one seemed to notice. They were a common-law married couple with three common-law children. Pariahs knew how it was, especially when Abner recommended that they form similar families to facilitate care of their orphaned children without social assistance from the larger normal communities. Because of course those communities tended to discriminate against Pariahs, leaving them to their own resources.

Then it happened. After a routine organizational session in a new town, Nefer spoke. "One of those children was a sopath."

"The leader's boy," Dreda agreed immediately. "He's going to rape some girl."

"The pretty little redhead," Clark said. "I saw him eying her."

"I wondered," Bunty said. "He reminded me of mine. I thought it was just a physical resemblance."

Yet Abner had not picked up on it. His sopath had been a girl. But he suspected it was more than that: the women and children of any age were more sensitive to the personal nuances, perhaps because they had more to fear from sopaths. Abner had been busy making his presentation, so really had not been looking; maybe he would have picked up on it otherwise. Yet the local Pariahs had been deceived, so it was more than merely gender or age. Abner's whole family was more attuned, especially the girls.

Abner put it into his daily report to Pariah, identifying the family and the boy. Pariah would handle it, probably by officially ignoring it. But they would be aware, and no really private information would go to that group, unless it was something they wanted sopaths to know.

It confirmed that sopaths could and did infiltrate Pariah groups without their knowledge. That could be mischief.

"Probably he's just hiding, to keep a good family," Clark said. "Stupid sopaths wreck things. Smart ones hide."

"Exactly," Nefer said, smiling at him. And Abner suffered another quiet shock: the boy tried to mute his reaction, but her smile had the impact of a kiss. Clark was beginning to like Nefer, despite knowing her nature.

Bunty had picked up on it too, as she murmured later that evening. "She's openly courting you, knowing we see it as futile. But she's not ignoring Clark. If she ever really wants something from him, she'll get it."

"By seducing him," Abner agreed morosely.

"We may once have thought that children have no interest in romance or sex. Now we know better, at least where sopaths are concerned. I don't think we can prevent it except by banishing her from the family. Do we even want to?"

"You mean, let her seduce him?"

"It would probably amount to no more than intimate peeks and feels. Hand on penis, finger in vagina. I did it as a child, and surely you did too. It's part of normal childhood curiosity, learning about the naughty parts. Maybe kisses. Pretending that she cares. That's how she gets her way with boys when she trades for information. She'll be doing that foraging for us, when we need her to. We know her nature; why not let her exercise it in positive ways?"

"But they're children!"

"We were speaking of naiveté."

She was right. He was being naïve. If Nefer was going to

seduce anyone, Clark was probably better than Abner himself. "Maybe our best course is to give her reason to keep it positive. To support the family, though I'm not sure how."

"If another sopath girl tried to seduce Clark, that could be lethal. Nefer could distract him from that worse threat."

"Maybe so," he agreed reluctantly. "Because Nefer probably won't hurt him. She's just shoring up her base."

"True."

They let it rest there, but Abner remained uneasy. They really did have a savage animal in their midst, behaving for now, but if that changed it could get extremely ugly in a hurry.

After a month on the road, during which they thoroughly polished their technique and identity as organizers, they came to the twin towns of Sweetpea and Sauerkraut. Abner felt an anticipatory chill, and knew the others did too.

"Remember," Abner said. "Officially we are nothing more than an organization advice group. Participate, observe, and do not react if you see something relevant. They may be testing us."

"Is there danger?" Clark asked, interested.

"There may be. Stay close to Bunty and me; don't get separated from us."

"But we doubt there's real physical danger," Bunty said reassuringly. "More likely we just won't find what we're looking for."

"What about bugs?" Nefer asked.

"Good question," Abner said, and saw her flush with pleasure. "If there is something going on, they could have mikes and cameras concealed everywhere. So from the time we enter either of those towns, assume someone is spying on us. Act normal. If you identify a sopath, ignore it until we're out of there."

"That's too late," Nefer said. "You need to be warned while it's happening."

He sighed. "Right again. Okay, let's set up a code. What can it be?"

"If we call you father and mother, instead of daddy and

mommy," Dreda said enthusiastically.

"And whatever we say next will be a lie," Clark said.

"I'll do it too," Nefer said. "I'll call you father and mother." She smiled almost wistfully. "I'd almost mean it. I like being with you, and not just because I want to get hold of Abner's penis."

"Daughters generally don't want to get hold of their father's penises," Abner said.

Now there was nothing wistful about her smile. "You think? If you could read Dreda's mind, would it be there?"

Dreda blushed. She was only five years old, but she knew. She must have had thoughts, and Nefer had picked up on them.

Abner exchanged a glance with Bunty. Nefer had set them back again. How many girls had Electra complexes to outgrow? How many boys similarly had Oedipus complexes? Did they really outgrow them, when so many married partners who resembled their opposite-gender parents? It was a sobering notion.

"So we have the code," Bunty said firmly. "No need to discuss it further."

Could that work? It was so simplistic as to be idiotic, but that might enable it to pass below the radar. "Okay."

"And I will call you Abner," Bunty said. "Instead of 'dear.' You can call me Bunty, similarly."

"We seem to have it," Abner agreed, bemused.

They reached Sweetpea in midafternoon and drove into a convenient motel. But when Abner sought to register at the front office, the clerk shook his head. "You are the Pariah organizer," he said. "There are better accommodations awaiting you at the Sweetpea Hotel."

"Oh, we don't seek anything special," Abner said, taken aback. Normally they were anonymous despite being open about his name, Abner Slate, because few in the larger community paid much attention to Pariahs, and generally avoided them anyway. "We can't afford anything fancy."

"The cost is covered by the town," the clerk assured him. "We want you to feel welcome here."

Abner distrusted this, but didn't want to make an issue. "Then we will gratefully accept, hoping it is not a case of misplaced identification. We're really pretty ordinary folk." What a whopper!

Soon enough they were ensconced in a luxurious suite complete with hot tub; kitchenette stocked with wine, beer, crackers, and chocolate milk; and a television in all five rooms. The children plunged into the hot tub while Abner and Bunty showered and changed. "It does seem like mistaken identity," Bunty murmured. "Somehow they got the notion that we're important."

"I hope there isn't a horrendous bill when they discover otherwise." They were being careful to be completely normal in their mild confusion, because if there was a reason for this treatment, it might be that the local authorities had caught on to their real mission. There was no sign of any electronic spying devices, but of course there wouldn't be.

In due course they all dried and changed into their good clothing, ready to contact the local Pariah chapter. Nefer was one of the children, perfectly emulating the excitement of the other two. None of them said anything important.

The phone rang. Abner answered it. "Mr. Slate, this is Mayor Jonathan Jones of Sweetpea Pariah. May we come to your suite to talk with you?"

"By all means!" Abner said warmly. "Maybe you can explain why we are being treated so much better than we deserve."

The man laughed. "Perhaps. Fifteen minutes?"

"Sure."

"If you need to use the bathroom, do it now," Abner told the children sternly. "We don't want to be fidgeting when company comes."

"We won't fidget," Dreda promised.

"Much," Clark said. "We'd rather watch that adult channel."

"No," Bunty said firmly. It was all part of their act for the cameras. The children were as curious as the adults were about this unusual treatment.

Jonathan Jones arrived promptly and was ushered in to the audience chamber. He was a large, bluff man with an ingratiating smile, a typical politician. Abner disliked him on sight, but suppressed his reaction as unreasonable.

Jones got straight to the point. "I instituted a local Pariah chapter because the sopath question is serious and we want it competently handled. We have no native sopaths here, but we do have survivors who fled from our neighbor town Sauerkraut. They can certainly use your help, and you will be meeting them soon. But I have a private concern."

"We will keep your secret," Abner said with a smile.

Jones did not smile in return. "I said private." He glanced meaningfully at the children.

"Our children are part of our family," Abner said. "They are survivors. They have experienced the worst. We do not hide things from them."

"You are unusual."

"We are united."

Jones looked uncomfortable, but proceeded. "I assume that your itinerary will take you next to Sauerkraut."

"It does," Abner agreed.

"Do not go there. It may be dangerous for you."

Well, now. "How so?"

"They have many sopaths there. In fact they pretty well run things. They desire to remain anonymous. If your visit threatens to compromise that anonymity, they would hardly hesitate to kill all of you."

Bunty made a sharp intake of breath, and the children began to cry. All part of the act. They knew that sopaths were dangerous, especially when challenged.

"I did request privacy," Jones reminded him. The man saw his caution vindicated.

"But we mean neither you nor them any harm," Abner protested. "All we want to do is help their local Pariah chapter get organized."

"Please do not play cute with me, Mr. Slate. You want to

know what's going on there. They can't afford to be exposed. Unless you can convince them, or allow me to convince them, that you do not intend to report to Pariah, entering Sauerkraut would be suicide. I will answer any questions you have, to the best of my ability, on the condition that our situation is not publicized."

"You are protecting the privacy of sopaths?" Abner asked.

"We have an understanding, and get along well with them. In fact, we handle the connections to the outside world, as they lack responsible adults. In return they provide labor and other services."

"Services?" Bunty asked, frowning.

"Maid services, mainly, by their teens. Sauerkraut has some older ones, but younger ones participate too."

"Sopaths?"

"They work for pay, just as others do."

"Others call it prostitution," Bunty said. "Just how old and young do they come?" Because of course the maids had to be underage. That didn't bother sopaths, but should have bothered the employers.

Jones spread his hands, embarrassed. He glanced at the children, but they did not move and neither Abner nor Bunty yielded. "Our children know about sopath sex," Abner said.

Jones shrugged and continued. "They are generally uneducated, and proffer what they can. Some are, um, aesthetic. There is a market. We do not inquire about the details."

"We are beginning to appreciate why you don't want your association of towns publicized," Abner said dryly.

"We are dealing with sopaths," Jones repeated. "They are not ordinary folk. We relate in what ways are feasible. It is mutually beneficial."

Abner was growing increasingly annoyed. The man was a stuffed shirt, covering for a reprehensible trade in young flesh. But there was no point in trying to make an issue. They were indeed sopaths, who had to be dealt with on their own terms, or killed.

"If I may," Bunty interposed, flashing a smile to melt the hardest heart. She was good at that. "We have a policy of not prying into sopath details either. But I am curious how you as mayor could have been victimized by a sopath."

Jones grimaced. "No secret. My son was an incorrigible brat. I thought he would grow out of it. I did not know about sopaths then."

"We, too," Bunty said. "My son burned down our house."

"We were driving to a key meeting. He refused to remain in the child harness. I rebuked him, then spanked him when he sassed me. I thought that would be the end of it, but when I resumed driving, he tore loose and attacked me. It was like having a vicious wild animal in my lap. I lost control of the car and we crashed. The boy was killed. So was my wife." He shook his head. "*Then* I learned about sopaths, thanks to Pariah. I hate them all." He took a breath. "But there are practical considerations, and the sopaths of Sauerkraut are disciplined and useful. As long as they remain that way, we tolerate them. In fact we do not need the participation of the national Pariah. We did not invite you here."

So the lavish welcome was indeed a way to try to buy them off, so they would depart without prying further.

"Nevertheless we of the national Pariah are dealing with sopaths too," Abner said. "We do understand. We are not here to expose titillating interactions. We want to tackle the larger picture, the very existence of sopaths, hoping to find a way to stop further sopath births. We will depart without awkwardness if you can clarify certain questions, so as to make further exploration unnecessary."

"Ask," Jones said tightly.

"How do you arrange to have no sopaths born in Sweetpea?"

"I can't answer that."

"Can't, or won't?"

"Mr. Slate, we simply do not know. We are blessed, and hope it remains that way. There is no secret method, no treatment or drug. We indulge normally, and no sopaths are born."

"What of the visiting sopath maids?" Bunty asked. "Don't some of them get pregnant?"

"Some do," Jones agreed reluctantly. "Those that are old enough." Which meant that those who were not old enough were also having sex. Abner understood, knowing Nefer. Age was no barrier to a sopath.

"Sopaths can't raise babies," Bunty said. "They would have no human love or patience, and the babies would soon die of neglect, or be beaten to death for crying. Do you allow that to happen?"

Jones looked distinctly uncomfortable. "We do not. Any who become pregnant here are allowed to remain here until they give birth. Then we take the babies and care for them."

"And these children of sopaths—souled or sopath?"

"Souled, always."

"So it's not the parentage," Abner said. "It must be the place."

"So it seems," Jones said. "We cannot explain it."

"And babies born in Sauerkraut?"

"Sopaths, almost always. Few survive long."

"Now this is significant," Abner said, excited. "This is the first we have seen of locality. Sopaths are normally born randomly, as we understand it, depending on the thinness of the available global soul supply. Why is it different here?"

"We do not know." Jones gestured with frustration. "But if the world knew, they would overwhelm us with pregnant visitors wanting to avoid the chance of giving birth to sopaths. We would be overrun, and our way of life destroyed. Surely you can appreciate our need for privacy."

"We can," Abner agreed. "But you can appreciate our need to solve the mystery. If there is something about Sweetpea that guarantees souls, and if we could discover it, we could make it available to the world and stop the sopath menace."

"There is nothing. We have searched. We are completely ordinary, geographically, as is Sauerkraut. There is nothing in the ground, air or water."

"But there is something," Abner said. "We have to discover what it is."

"Something different between the two towns," Bunty said. "We must identify that difference."

"Which means we have to move on to Sauerkraut," Abner concluded.

"They are no more eager to have the world know than we are," Jones said desperately. "The rush would expose them and destroy them also."

"They want to keep on birthing sopaths?"

"No! Sopaths don't want more sopaths. In fact they don't much want pregnancy, either. They endure it here only because we provide the prospective mothers with excellent care for the duration, and they don't have to work. We do it for the sake of their coming souled babies."

"They don't use contraceptives?" Bunty asked.

"They don't have the patience for them. They just want to do what is fun, or what pays, and ignore any likely consequences. They are completely irresponsible."

"And what of your residents, who are using them for sex," Abner said. "They don't take precautions either?"

"They are supposed to. Some have religious objections." Which was perhaps a sufficient answer. The residents of Sweetpea might have souls, but they were no more responsible than anyone else. No more moral, either. Their religion forbade them using contraception, but not fornicating with children? Indeed, there was nothing special about this town.

"But if we solved the mystery, wouldn't the sopaths benefit too?" Bunty asked.

"They may not care to look that far ahead."

Which was the problem with sopaths. "I believe we will have to go on to Sauerkraut," Abner said. "But we appreciate your warning. Now let's get on to organizing your local Pariah chapter."

"Can you at least commit to not spreading the word about Sweetpea's lack of sopath births?"

"Pariah already knows," Abner said. "But we have no interest in complicating your existence. We will let that aspect be, if possible."

"Thank you. I will guide you to the assembly, which is ready for your attention."

Soon they were in the gym where a number of people had gathered: men, women, children. A typical Pariah group. They applauded politely as Abner's family entered.

Abner introduced himself and his family, and his mission to organize them into a chapter in touch with the national Pariah organization, and the family sang a folk song. That put the survivors in the mood, as it always did, because of Nefer's magical voice. It was routine, and they were responsive. It seemed the mayor spoke only for himself in not wanting wider participation.

Then Abner plunged in to his real mission. "I understand that no sopaths are born in Sweetpea, and that all of you are refugees from Sauerkraut, where many sopaths are born." He saw many nods of agreement. "You are a larger group than I usually encounter, so I will introduce my family, then we'll break into two groups so that we can give attention to twice as many people in the time we have. Tomorrow we'll be moving on to Sauerkraut." He spoke casually, but was watching carefully for reaction.

He got it. "Don't go there," a woman said. "There are no Pariahs there. They are controlled by sopaths, and they can be vicious when crossed. We know." Several others nodded agreement. They had encountered not only sopaths in their families, but sopaths in the town government, surely a horror. Their best course had been to flee.

"I'm sure you do," Abner said. "But we are on the trail of a mystery: why are no sopaths born here in Sweetpea, and many born in Sauerkraut? We need to find out, and if we can't get the answer here, we must go there."

She was silent. The others looked nervous. They really were wary of Sauerkraut, for good reason.

He gave general advice on forming a full chapter and ad hoc temporary families, then split the family. Bunty and Clark would work with those interested in setting up a charter school, while he, Dreda, and Nefer would advise on instituting a non-denominational religious service.

When he had his group, he demonstrated how to do a hymn. This was where Nefer performed solo. She sang angelically, enchanting everyone present, as she always did. It motivated them to have choir.

But in the brief interim while they were discussing it, Dreda and Nefer approached him. "Father," Dreda said. "They want another hymn."

"Father, I will be glad to sing another," Nefer said.

They were both giving the signal. There was a sopath in this group.

"Who?" he asked tightly.

They indicated a five year old red-headed girl standing beside her red-headed mother. "Mother doesn't know," Nefer said.

"I'll see what I can do," Abner said. "Carry on here for a moment."

The girls shrugged. They were relating to the children, explaining that yes, adopted parents could be good parents, especially when they had been through the same horrors as the children.

Abner walked to Mayor Jones. "There is a sopath here," he murmured.

He reacted exactly as Abner had. "Who?"

"The girl beside the redhead there."

"Oh, no! I am courting that woman. Their sopath girl put rat poison in their food, killing her husband and other daughter."

Abner made an internal whistle. *It was the sopath who had survived, framing the souler sister for the crime.*

"It is not necessarily bad news," Abner said carefully. "Consistent firm discipline can civilize a sopath, and they can be useful, as your townsmen have discovered with the sopath maids."

"The sopaths from Sauerkraut are under Sauerkraut sopath discipline, which is deadly. Fear keeps them in line. But a sopath in a Pariah family? This would be extremely awkward."

"It doesn't have to be."

Jones shook his head. "Are you sure you know a sopath when you see one? I have had experience with sopaths, but have not seen the signs in that girl."

"They can masquerade as soulers," Abner said. "If they choose to. Smart ones are more likely to, because they realize it is dangerous to be exposed as a sopath."

"You must be mistaken." The man was in denial.

"Perhaps I should demonstrate," Abner said. "I have a sopath in my own family."

"You must be joking."

"Nefer, here."

"The angelic soloist? I can't believe it."

Abner beckoned, and the girl came over. "Tell him, Nefer."

"I am a sopath."

"I don't believe it. You appreciate beauty and religion. You sang a wonderful hymn."

"I don't give a shit about religion," she said sweetly. "Or about what you believe, pecker-head. If you want, I will strip naked and masturbate myself in public while singing another hymn. I'll tell them you made me do it."

"You wouldn't dare!"

Nefer started singing another hymn, her voice as beautiful as ever. As she sang, she started unbuttoning her dress and gyrating suggestively. All eyes turned toward her, as the hymn attracted attention.

"All right, all right, desist," Jones said quickly. "You made your point."

Nefer glanced at Abner. He nodded.

She continued singing, but stopped the other actions.

There was applause as she finished the hymn. She made a little appreciative curtsy, looking impossibly angelic. "Thank you for asking, Mr. Jones," she said, blushing. Abner had not realized she could fake even that. The others returned to their other activities.

"Heaven and hell," Jones said, daunted. "And she obeys you implicitly, showing no fear. How do you do it?"

"She loves me," Abner said.

"Sopaths don't love!"

"You would call it lust," Nefer said. "I'm hot for him and want him to fuck me. He knows it and uses it to control me with the hint that he might be weakening. If I push it too hard, too soon, he'll kill me. He's one tough stud." She smiled longingly at Abner.

Jones was taken aback. "Do sopath girls actually feel sexual desire? I assumed they tolerate some of our men only for the sake of the food and money."

"We can be horny as hell," Nefer said. "With the right man. We'd as soon kill the wrong man. So you're right: they're selling the fucks for cash, but maybe after a few times some of them are getting to like the men. It's a two way street. We don't need souls to like a good cock."

Jones evidently had a horrible thought. "That girl you say is a sopath. She has seen me kissing her mother. What would be her motive with respect to me?"

"Chances are she's seen you fuck her mother, too, and she wants a piece of it. But mostly she knows she'll always be safe if you marry her mother, so she'll behave until you do. Then she'll see about seducing you herself. You bet she knows what the Kraut girls are doing."

"I would never—she's only five years old!"

"Here's how it's done, dope. She'll come to you when you're alone, and ask you to fuck her, carefully. Maybe just stroking your cock along her wet little slit, the first time. If you do, she'll enjoy it and keep her mouth shut. If you don't, she'll scream and tell her mother and the world you tried to rape her.

She'll be damned persuasive. You won't be mayor long after that." Nefer half smiled. "So you had better do it. It's easier all around. She'll play along as long as you behave. You might even like it. Many men do."

"This is appalling!"

"No problem," Nefer said. "Kill her, or don't marry her mother. Maybe arrange to have the sopath have a fatal accident while you're out of town, so you won't be blamed. Then her mother's safely yours. Fuck her all you want."

Jones looked at Abner. "You tolerate this creature in your family?"

"We're dealing with sopaths," Abner said seriously. "We need to understand them. This is the way they think and act. That's another reason we'll be moving on to Sauerkraut."

"Do that tomorrow," Jones said grimly. "I wash my hands of it." He walked away.

"That was fun," Nefer said. "Thanks for letting me, Abner."

Abner squeezed her shoulder. "Actually, it *was* fun. He's such a self-important shirt. You took him down."

"Any time, Abner. I love you, and it's not all lust. Mostly, but not all."

"I believe it."

They carried through on the organization routine, but knew that their welcome was now quite limited. Jones would not talk about it, but he would want nothing more to do with them. They had become pariahs even among Pariahs. Abner made a quiet phone report to Pariah. They had learned significant things, but the main mystery remained.

"I am nervous about tomorrow," Bunty said as they turned in. "In fact I'm terrified. The prospect of dealing with teen-aged sopaths is daunting."

"I can go in alone," Abner said.

"No. I'm scared for you as much as for the family."

"We're all scared," Clark said. "But we know we've got to do it." Dreda nodded agreement. They were young, but they had the courage of conscience.

"So am I," Nefer said. "Sopaths can be scared too. I've got a notion what I'll be like as a teen, and that scares me. And I want to say this: if I think they're going to kill you, Abner, I will say or do anything to save you. So don't believe me, especially if I call you father."

"And if you think they're going to kill Bunty, Clark, or Dreda?" he asked.

"If I have to turn them in to save you, I will. But since I know that would forever poison any chance I have with you, I won't do it unless there's no other way."

Abner was shaken despite himself. "Maybe we should cancel."

"No," Bunty said firmly. "This is something we all have to do. We will live or die pursuing our mission." The two children grimly nodded agreement.

"Damn, I wish I could feel what you're feeling," Nefer said. "Before we all die."

"Then you wouldn't be a sopath," Clark reminded her.

"Damn," Nefer repeated morosely. That seemed to sum it all up.

CHAPTER 8

The outlying environment of Sauerkraut reminded Abner of militarily occupied territory. Three quarters of the farm houses were shuttered, their yards overgrown, obviously unoccupied. Many of their fields were fallow. The occupied and maintained ones stood out like ragged islands.

"This is grim," Bunty remarked.

"When a hostile force occupies a region, in war, the natives have to flee or accommodate," Abner said. "I have seen it. There is no point in stopping at any house; they will be afraid of us, or of retaliation if they show us any courtesy. We shall have to deal directly with the conquerors."

"Which will be sopaths."

"Yes."

"They have to know we're coming, and our mission."

"Yes. We're like a foreign embassy entering under flag of truce. They may not honor it."

"They will for a while," Nefer said. "They'll know you are coming in for a reason, and they'll want to know that reason. Otherwise you could have skipped the town."

"But will they believe that we just want to solve the riddle of the twin towns, and maybe fathom the secret of sopath births?"

"Maybe." Abner brought out his cell phone and called Pariah. "We are nearing the target. Is the unit in place and zeroed in?"

"It is. Response will be thirty seconds from your directive. First one a warning, second one for effect."

"Good enough," Abner said. "I suspect we'll need it."

"Unit?" Bunty asked.

"Military hardware I asked them to set up overnight. We're not playing games here."

"Indeed we are not," she agreed.

"Background for the rest of you," Abner said. "It seems that Sauerkraut is governed by a teen-aged female sopath named Topsy, said to be as beautiful and vicious as they come."

"Topsy?" Clark asked. "What's she doing with a cute name?"

"You never can tell," Nefer said. "I chose mine because I heard of Queen Nefertiti and it also sounds like Never. She has to have some nasty reason."

"Surely so," Abner agreed. "She came to power about a year ago, ruthlessly eliminating competitors. She's young but smart, and it seems knows how to make people do her bidding. She rewards grown souler men with sex, and grown souler women with other favors, such as getting the men of their choice. The men's first desire is for Topsy, but they know they won't get any part of her unless they obey her whims, so they settle for the other women when Topsy tells them to. It's cynical but effective."

"She's a sopath, all right," Nefer said. "Are you sure you can handle her, Abner? She'll be worse than me."

"Pariah seems to think that I can."

"It's his secret weapon," Bunty said. "Personal magnetism, otherwise known as raw sex appeal. Women of any age are attracted to him. You may have noticed."

Nefer and Dreda laughed. They had noticed.

"I will have to get her close to me and keep her there for a while," Abner said. "I will try to play it straight, presenting my mission, but if that doesn't work, we'll just have to hope that the secret weapon, as Bunty puts it, does. There is a serious risk regardless. We can still turn back."

"No," the children said together.

"I'm not sure you're considering just how ugly it may become."

"Daddy, we know about sopaths," Dreda said bravely.

Abner let it drop, hoping this deadly gamble would play out successfully. The family had seen less of the viciousness of sopaths than he had.

There was a structure ahead. It turned out to be a check point, covered by a machine gun. Abner glided up to it and stopped.

"Who are you?" the young teen guard demanded.

"I am Abner Slate, representing Pariah. This is my family."

"Why are you here?"

"There is a mystery about Sweetpea and Sauerkraut. No sopaths are born there, and few soulers here. We want to know why."

"Yeah?"

"Yeah."

The kid consulted briefly on his cell phone. That sort of thing was of course part of what the sopaths needed money for. They might have preferred to be completely isolated from the rest of the world, but had discovered that this was not feasible.

Then he evidently got his orders. "Get out of the car."

Rather than try to argue with possibly trigger-happy minions, Abner obliged. "Do it," he murmured.

The five of them got out. They were marched to an adjacent building and separated. None of them offered any resistance.

Abner found himself in a chamber by himself. He sat and waited about half an hour. He knew they would get around to him soon enough. They had to bring in their authorities. Topsy herself, with luck.

A gruff older man entered. "You're no sopath," Abner said.

"I work for them," the man said.

"I'll bet." The fact that a person had a soul did not guarantee he would be ethical or independent. Sex and threats could be powerful persuaders.

"Now here's the situation," the man said. "You came to spy on us and mess us up. What we want to know is why. Tell us, and maybe you'll see your family again."

Abner remembered military interrogation procedures. This

was not very sophisticated. "We came to find out why so many sopaths are born here."

"You lie."

Uh-huh. He was definitely dealing with amateurs. "What is the basis of this charge?"

"We got it from your two younger children."

And doubtless lying similarly to the others about what Abner said. Standard operating procedure. "I doubt it. What of the older girl?"

"She collapsed in tears before we even asked."

That just might be true. Nefer was playing a dangerous game with them. Evidently they hadn't recognized her as a sopath herself. They surely would before long, however. "And what of my wife?"

"She clammed up. But she'll squeal soon enough when we torture the children."

There was the threat. They were clumsy, but had the essence. "You won't be doing that."

"Why not?"

"Because the moment you do, I'll be annoyed." Abner smiled. "You wouldn't like me when I'm annoyed."

The man frowned. "You're some joker, you know that?"

"This has gone far enough. Bring us back together, unharmed. We're here to meet with your superiors."

"Oh? And what if we don't?"

Abner moved too quickly for the man to react. In an instant he had him in a firm headlock. "That would annoy me."

The man tried to cry out, but Abner cut off his wind with a twist of his wrist against the windpipe. "I could kill you in a few seconds. But you're not worth bothering with. You're just a flunky. Now call your supervisor in here." He eased up a little.

"The hell!"

Abner shifted his grip slightly. Now it was a pain hold. "I didn't hear that. Will you cooperate?"

"The—"

This time the pain hold made the man groan in agony. "Do

I have to reach him over your dead body? Now get in line and I'll let you go."

The man took a moment to recover. Then he called "Autopsy! He's got me in a hold."

Abner was about to make him hurt again. But then a young woman appeared. "I will take it from here, Jud," she said.

So the mistress of Kraut really had come. That was a break. Not the childish Topsy, but the brutally suggestive Autopsy. As Nefer had said: she must have her reason. Maybe it was to make her seem less threatening to outsiders, while insiders knew how vicious she was.

Abner let the man go. He scrambled to his feet and out the door. Abner was left with the woman.

And what a woman she was. Her face was lovely almost beyond description, perfectly made up. She wore a low cut gown that showed more than half of her rouged breasts. Her fair hair was bound with a sparkling jeweled comb. She took a seat on the chair and crossed her right leg over the left not at the knee but midway along the calf so that her shapely thigh was exposed all the way to the buttock. The effect was compelling. This was like Nefer on steroids. "I am Autopsy," she said.

"You're a teen sopath!" Abner said, affecting surprise. She looked seventeen but was surely younger.

She leaned forward, showing more of her breasts. "Don't fool with me, Abner Slate. I saw you coming. Tell me what I want to know and I will let you touch me."

"We are here to try to discover why one town has no sopath births while the other has mostly sopath births. That could have global significance. Tell me that and I will leave you alone."

"You understand of course that we will not hesitate to torture your wife and children to death in front of you. Or to reward you with a fantastic experience if you cooperate."

She was speaking literally, but it was not his role to be cowed. "Cut out the threats and temptations, Autopsy. I will not be moved by either."

"Oh? I am curious to verify your constancy. Perhaps I will

strip us both naked and sit on your lap and fondle your penis while we watch the smallest girl writhe and scream as we burn out her eyes with red-hot pokers. Which distraction will interest you more?"

She wasn't bluffing. She was a sopath with power. It was time to halt this. "Here is why you won't do any of that. I have been in constant touch with the Pariah home office via a private signal you can't intercept. The moment I give the word, or cease to communicate, they will alert the state authorities who will do what they have been eager to do: raid you and kill all of you as rogue sopaths. All they need is a pretext, and I am that pretext. I will see that they capture rather than kill you personally, and if any of my family have been harmed, I will hold you securely bound and naked on my lap as I rape you with the hot poker you have prepared for my daughter. I suspect your body will writhe and scream in a most interesting manner."

She gazed at him, unconcerned. "I wonder."

"It is simple enough to have the proof of my threat. Start your torture."

"I think you're bluffing. You're a man, so you desire me and want to have sex with me. You're a souler, so you don't like hurting people, while it doesn't bother us at all."

"You are the one bluffing, bitch. You have no interest in torturing anyone unless you have something to gain by it. I, in contrast, care about my family, and will be motivated by vengeance. When the raid manifests you will flee to try to save your own hide, while I will make good on my threat. There's nothing quite as vicious as a motivated souler with a hard military background."

"That is true. We have some here." She studied him thoughtfully. "What do you want?"

"I want the answer to my question. Give it to me and I will leave you alone and see that Pariah does too. That's a bargain for you."

"We don't *have* the answer!" she snapped, her poise beginning to fray.

"I'll be damned. You mean it."

"Yes I mean it! All we want is to be left alone. We can't give you what you want."

Abner wasn't sure whether she was lying, because to sopaths the truth was merely one option among many. This still needed to be played out. "Then I can't give *you* what you want. We may simply have to clean you out and start over here with a study group."

She sighed. "Well, I tried to make nice. Now we'll do it my way. Follow me." She got up and walked out of the room.

Abner followed, involuntarily admiring her flexing buttocks under the tight skirt. He could have caught her and subdued her with a pain hold, but was pretty sure that would not work a second time. Her guards would instantly appear with guns. Her very ability to turn her back on him showed her confidence in her own safety.

They came to a larger room. There was Dreda, tied naked to a board. "Daddy!" she cried hopefully.

Abner saw that Bunty, Clark, and Nefer were seated on chairs across the room, facing the torture site. They were all naked, and all looked grim. They had evidently been told the same thing he had.

There were four male guards armed with knives, standing to the sides of the room. The thing about knives was that they were better for stages of torture than guns were. A gun was either fired or not fired, while a knife could cut off small sections at a time.

"We shall sit and watch the persuasion," Autopsy said. "Strip and sit, Abner Slate." She indicated a chair for him at the near end of the row.

She was inadvertently playing into his hands.

Abner removed his clothing and took the seat, retaining only the cell phone in his left hand. The fact that they had not taken it indicated either their confidence or their caution.

Autopsy stripped also and stood before him for a moment gloriously nude. Then she sat on his lap, her plush buttocks pressing warmly against his thighs. She reached down between her spread thighs, and took hold of his penis, exactly as she had threatened. She massaged it, and it hardened in her hand. It was now erect between her thighs. She had ferocious sex appeal, an animal magnetism that her mere appearance could not entirely account for. He abhorred the necessity of being so close to this vicious creature, yet his body was reacting forcefully. No wonder she governed here!

"So you're doing exactly what you threatened to," Abner said, keeping his voice calm.

"Exactly," she agreed sweetly, giving his penis a pull. "I am turned on by torture. How about you?"

"I will not allow it."

Autopsy glanced at the guards. "Proceed," she said.

One of the guards left the room. He returned a moment later with a poker that glowed red at its business end. It had been in a fire, made ready for this ugly use. He advanced on Dreda.

"All you need to do is promise to leave here and be silent about our control of this town," Autopsy murmured in his ear. "I know that as a Pariah official you will keep your word in a way a sopath would not."

"I will keep my given word," he agreed. "I have not given it except in this respect: Your doom is sealed the moment that poker touches my child."

"And when you do promise, not only will she go free unharmed, but I will give you the fuck of your life." She reached down to catch his right hand and bring it to her bare right breast. She pressed it in, causing it to massage the flesh. His estimate had been correct: she was like Nefer on steroids. There was the same kind of animal magnetism about her that others had described about him, and he desired her fiercely.

"It will not be my penis that enters you," he said, though his member was now rigid and on the verge of jettisoning. She was a sopath, but she had one of the finest bodies he had ever encountered, and she knew it. She must have achieved her position among sopaths, including the girls, by being the most physically attractive.

The man pointed the poker at Dreda's face and pushed it slowly forward, centering on her left eye. Terrified, she urinated on the floor.

Abner watched. He had to keep Autopsy close to him as long as possible, hoping that Pariah's confidence in his secret weapon was not misplaced. That meant allowing this revolting challenge to proceed until his hand was forced. Dreda had depended on him to protect her, and he intended to do that, but she was in serious doubt now. How he wished he could reassure her!

Autopsy put her thighs together, squeezing his turgid member between them. How well she knew her power! "Desire is beating horror," she remarked. "So far."

"You can't bluff him," Nefer said. "Under that souler mask there's one extremely tough man."

"We shall see," Autopsy said, tightening her thighs to put additional pressure on his penis.

There needed to be a more immediate show of force. "Deliver the warning shell," Abner said into the phone.

"How long before detonation?" Autopsy inquired as if it were routine. She must have let him keep the phone so she could call his bluff.

"About thirty seconds."

"Wait thirty seconds," she told the poker bearer.

He held the poker in place, about two inches before Dreda's eye. She was quietly sobbing, fearing the worst.

Then the shell exploded in the intersection outside the house with an authoritative boom. The building rattled.

"I'll be damned," Autopsy said, startled. He felt it in her momentary clench of thighs, and pause of breath beneath her breast. "You do have us covered."

"Did you think I walked into this nest of scorpions, with my family, unprepared?" Abner asked rhetorically. "We of Pariah do know something about handling sopaths."

She remained on his lap, reassessing the situation. "So it seems. We have guards to stop anyone from driving or walking in. How did you get the bomb there, and set it off?"

"It's a mortar," Abner said. "That's a mini-cannon that hurls shells in a high arc, to land and detonate like bombs. You can't defend against it. We have it zeroed in on this site. The next round will be for effect."

"You'd bomb yourself and your family to get at us? I don't think so."

"When the alternative is torture? We'll soon know, won't we?" Abner asked, squeezing her breast a bit too hard. He could merge sadism with sex when he chose to. He needed her to accept that he was indeed a tough man.

"Then we'd better get on with it." Autopsy glanced at the poker man and opened her mouth.

Abner raised the phone to his face. Bluff and counter bluff, not about their abilities, but their nerve. If Autopsy thought she could still make Abner yield, she would. But she didn't want to have that poker raping her, and he didn't want to have to do it. But he could, and would. He was already furious about the way Dreda was being terrorized.

Autopsy slapped the phone out of his hand. It dropped to the floor and skidded before the chairs. Bunty dived for it, but a guard intercepted her and held her tightly against him. He was evidently eager to rape her the moment he was given leave.

Clark tried for the phone, but another guard kicked it back the way it had come. Autopsy slid off Abner's lap, reached lithely down, and scooped it up.

Only to discover herself caught from behind, with a knife at her throat. While the others had focused on the phone, Nefer had focused on Autopsy. "Try to bluff *me*, cow!" she hissed.

The guards, seeing their mistress captive, froze in place. The poker retreated from Dreda's face. Abner retrieved the phone from Autopsy's hand. She had lost their contest of wills, by not letting him call in the strike.

"You're a sopath!" Autopsy said, amazed. "You serve a souler?"

Nefer shrugged without letting the knife blade waver. "There's just something about him. I love him."

"And he keeps you in his family? You must be one hell of a young fuck!"

"I am, but he doesn't know it yet." She looked at Abner. "Do I kill her? You know we can't trust her. Those goons won't wait forever without orders."

Abner hesitated deliberately. "You kill her, you take her place," he said. "It's the way an anarchist society works. They'll obey you. It could be a good deal for you. A sopath-controlled town. Power and an easy life."

"Yes, but I'll still serve you, and you won't want to stay here. There's nothing I want here, when you go. I'd be in constant fear of getting knocked off by the next power-hungry sopath bitch."

Abner made his decision. "Then let her go. We already have the situation in hand, and she could be useful."

"She could also be one really hot fuck," Nefer agreed, slowly releasing the woman. "She's got the body I don't have yet."

Right on target. Abner's erection remained, in plain sight of everyone, desiring the sopath leader even now. He had underestimated her sheer sexual appeal.

Autopsy got to her feet. "Loose the child," she said to the guards. "Then get out of here. The issue has been settled; the operation is under new management." She turned to Abner, inhaling. "Tell your mortar crew to ease off. We don't want some trigger-happy joker shelling this house while we're in it. We haven't fucked yet." She glanced at his stiff penis, knowing that this aspect of her power remained. Like Nefer, she could bide her time when she needed to.

Abner lifted his cell phone and did so. Meanwhile the guards freed Dreda, and she came running across to Abner. He swept her up and held her tightly, comforting her as she sobbed. She had known he would protect her if he could, but had not been sure he could. He had not been sure either, if his threat did not dissuade the sopath.

"You're right," Autopsy said to Nefer. "There's something about him. Just being close to him makes me want to fuck him." Which was her way of saying that she was getting a crush on him, as Nefer had. It seemed that sopaths had no natural limitations apart from conscience; when they got turned on by someone, they plunged in all the way in mere minutes. That could be a worthwhile lever, and was in this case. Pariah had gambled on it and on him to implement it, and won. Autopsy wanted sex with him, yes, but this was beyond that, and would not end if she seduced him. Exactly as Nefer had discovered.

"He has that effect," Bunty said.

"But there's one thing I don't get," Autopsy said. "I know why you made her let me go, Abner, because I made your penis hot and you really want that fuck. All men do. You just want to fuck me on your own terms, not mine. It's a power thing. But you, Nefer—you're a sopath like me, and you want to fuck him too. You could have saved the competition by killing me. He gave you leave to do it. You know I can seduce him before you can, because I've got the hardware you lack, and once he fucks me, he'll have no interest in you. Why did you throw away your chance like that?"

"Because I love him," Nefer said. "I'll do anything he wants me to. So will you. He's got the power."

Autopsy surveyed Abner again. "He does. I've never felt anything like this. Fucking's always been a business for me, and I'm good at it. I've fucked every man in Kraut, most of them multiple times. They can never get enough of me. All I ever felt before for a man was contempt. A man will throw away everything just to get his penis into my slit before it bursts. Just to pump his gism into me. I enjoy sex but it doesn't govern me like that. That's weakness."

"Abner won't. He has this thing about not fucking children."

"So I have discovered. But I'm not a child, just young. I

made him hard, but I didn't make him try to get into me. He's strong. I think he really would have raped me with that poker if I hurt his child. I admire that. But this is more. I want him to *want* me. I want him to possess me. I want him to—to love me."

"That's the hell of it," Nefer said. "He won't. He hates sopaths, and usually kills them. He loves Bunty, and she's the only one he'll fuck, and if anyone touches her or the children he'll kill them. I've worked with him; I know. Love is like a magic spell cast over you that you can't fight. You don't even *want* to fight it. You just want to be with him and do anything he wants you to, knowing you'll never get any more than the satisfaction of pleasing him."

"That is weird." Autopsy shook her head. "But true. It's the way the men are with me. I wanted to get close to him the moment I saw him."

"Yep," Nefer agreed. "You thought you were seducing him, but he was seducing you, not for sex, but for love, which is worse. And *that's* why I made him let you go. Now you're his captive, his love slave, same as me, and if there's any way you can be useful, you'll do it. You must know a lot about this place. Maybe you'll help us complete our mission."

Nefer smiled. "For that, maybe he just might fuck you, if Bunty tells him to. Just as he'd fuck me, if she told him to. It's a faint hope, but it's all there is."

Autopsy glanced at Bunty, who nodded.

"Weird," Autopsy repeated. She seemed to be in a partial daze, overwhelmed by the unfamiliar emotion. For the first time in her life she wanted to give rather than to take. It was contrary to her sopath nature.

Nefer had done Abner the favor of clarifying Autopsy's new-found loyalty to him. It was time for him to take over. He held Dreda close and spoke over her head. "Autopsy, I am leaving you in command of Sauerkraut, under me," he said. "I could have killed you at any time, or shelled the house, but wanted to play out the scene. Are you satisfied that your choices are to obey me and live, or oppose me and die?"

"Not entirely, because if it weren't for this emotion, this love, I could get rid of you soon enough. This is my town. But I do want to fuck you, and to make you like me. Give me that, and I'll do what else you say, no limits, as she says."

Abner answered cautiously, aware that this extremely attractive sopath was now dangerous in other than a purely physical way. When he saw her torturing Dreda he hated her, but now she was on his side. Nefer had slowly gotten him to like her, and Autopsy was apt to do the same despite his knowledge of her vicious nature. "Not at this time. You will have to satisfy me that you are sufficiently useful for my purpose. That may take time."

"See?" Nefer said. "He's playing you as he plays me, and you know it, but all you can do is beg for more."

Autopsy nodded. "Just let me be close to you, Abner. I'm not used to this, but I'm a quick study."

She surely was, to have survived and achieved power as a teen. She had made expert use of her power over men. "I want your full effort to fathom the mystery of these two towns," he said. "To figure out why the one has no sopath births while the other has mostly sopath births. If we can get that answer, I will probably depart and leave you here as you were, giving you what you want."

"I don't want it anymore," Autopsy said. "I want to go with you, as Nefer does." She smiled with a suggestion of humor. "To be your love slave." She glanced at Bunty. "Your concubine, for when your wife's not in the mood. I am always in the mood."

"I can't promise that."

"Or have you stay here, and work with you. Just so long as it's close to you."

Abner was surprised. "That might be possible, depending on what we discover. We do need a new place to settle."

"I'll try as hard as I possibly can," Autopsy promised. "Anything I know, anything I can get for you, it's yours."

"That should suffice."

"Kiss her," Nefer advised, satisfied with the way of it. "To seal the deal."

Abner glanced at Bunty, who nodded again. So he took Autopsy in his arms and kissed her on the lips. He felt her melting. He had indeed made another conquest.

She remained infernally tempting. How long would he be able to hold out against her seduction?

After that they all dressed and adjourned to more comfortable quarters. The guards were gone, food was served, and Autopsy was resplendent in a more modest dress that hardly masked her beauty. She looked like the world's loveliest Girl Back Home. It was hard to believe that she had sat naked on his lap while fondling his penis, or that she had ordered Dreda tortured. Dreda, however, refused to look at her. Her second brush with a hostile sopath had not been any more pleasant than her first.

"I am convinced that the secret is hiding in plain sight," Abner said. "Maybe if we review the history of the two towns we'll happen upon it." He looked at Autopsy. "You must have been close to the first sopath born here. I am not inquiring into your personal history, merely the larger situation. When did the sopaths start?"

"I could have been the first," she agreed. "My family was the first to move here after the fruities left, and I was born soon after."

"Fruities?"

"The cult freaks. Their canon was to be fruitful and multiply, like in the Bible, and did they ever! I think they just liked to fuck. They thought nothing of having ten or twelve children in a family. Their women were almost continuously pregnant, including the single ones."

"Then they left," Bunty said. "Somewhat abruptly, I understand. Why?"

"No one knows. They seemed to be doing great, then suddenly they moved far far away, leaving their houses empty.

Something must've scared them off, like a toxic nuclear waste dump buried under the town, poisoning everything. Except it wasn't. My folks checked that out, before I ditched them. No waste, no radiation. The environment was fine, and nobody since has suffered any problems. The town's clean, except for the sopaths."

"Much of it looked deserted as we drove in," Abner said. "Empty houses, fallow fields, as if a blight struck it."

Autopsy laughed. "That was us. The sopaths. We did so much damage that folk started moving out as fast as they had moved in. So now we're trying to get more settlers in, especially responsible older soulers, but they're wary. I could persuade the men, but their wives won't let them be within a hundred miles of here. So there's just not enough people here."

"While there are plenty in Sweetpea," Bunty said. "And work for visiting sopaths too."

"We need the money. We put the fear of hell into any soaps we send there, so they behave. Anything the Sweets want, we'll provide if we can, for cash."

Soap? A nickname for sopath. Abner knew the children would pick right up on it.

"So we understand," Bunty said. "Including child prostitutes."

"Sure. Why not? There's a market."

"The question is," Abner reminded them, "why the disparity in sopath births. How do the two towns differ?"

Autopsy shrugged. "Got me. They had that slaughter, then nothing."

Something jogged Abner's mind. "Kraut had huge families, while Sweet had half its population wiped out a few years later. Is there a connection?"

"The fruities," Clark said. "Did they have sopaths?"

"Dunno," Autopsy said. "I hear they were close-mouthed about personal things."

"It was really before the time of the sopaths," Abner said. "You're the oldest sopath we have encountered."

"This just seems to be the place for us," Autopsy agreed.

"I wonder," Bunty said. "Abner, you mused on whether there could be a connection between Sweetpea's tragedy and Sauerkraut's fertile cultists. The one town had a serious loss of population, while the other was rapidly gaining. Could Kraut have simply run out of available souls?"

"More would have been drawn in from elsewhere," Abner said.

"Are we sure of that? How long does it take for souls to find their hosts? Maybe it's not instantaneous."

"I'm not clear what you're getting at."

"Are souls like little clouds?" Clark asked. "Drifting?"

That made it come together for Abner. "A soul without a host—how does it travel? It has no legs or wings, I think."

"Clouds go where the wind goes," Clark said. "I've watched them."

"And what wind moves spirits without substance?" Bunty asked.

It was coming together. "They could simply remain where they are, where people died and left them," Abner said. "Maybe spreading out a bit, but not moving far. So where many people die, like in a hospital, there could be many souls."

"Many births occur in hospitals," Bunty said. "Probably more than deaths. No surplus of souls there."

"Sweetpea!" Clark said. "Half the people died! Big pile of souls!"

"And Sauerkraut," Bunty said. "Where the fruities used up all the souls."

"The bastards!" Autopsy swore. "I was born in a damn vacuum!"

"While if your folks had moved to Sweetpea, you'd have had a soul," Clark said, pleased with himself for discovering it.

"I believe we've got it," Abner said. "The locality of souls. Where we lived it was residential, with a good birth rate and the few who died moved first to retirement communities elsewhere. So we had an increasing number of sopaths."

"If I had known," Bunty said soberly, "I'd have visited a retirement community to give birth."

"But you know, it won't last," Abner said. "Soon enough those extra souls in Sweetpea will be used up, and then they'll be just like other places."

"So we have a formidable insight," Bunty agreed. "But not a solution."

"That comes next," Abner said.

CHAPTER 9

They pondered it the next few hours. Autopsy turned out to be a good hostess, having accepted the new reality, and they had an excellent hotel suite. They were sure it was bugged, but didn't care.

"It's only because she loves you, father," Nefer said as they relaxed before the TV in the evening. "She wants you to be pleased with her, and to stay here. She knows she can't stop you from leaving, and that you're not going to take her into your family the way you did me, and anyway, she'd lose her base if she left here. She has to fuck those men regularly or they'll start getting restive." What she said seemed true, but her use of the term father signaled that it was false. She thought Autopsy was faking her conversion. Abner agreed. They had handled only the first round of their encounter.

"That makes me wonder, Abner," Bunty said. "She said she has had sex with all the local men, and we have no reason to doubt it, because it's how she maintains control. So why isn't she pregnant? She surely doesn't use any contraceptives." Again, what she said made sense, but she didn't trust the situation.

"That's right," Abner agreed. "We know sopaths can get pregnant, because the ones that service Sweetpea men do. And what about VD? In any large group of men, that's bound to exist."

"Daddy, what's veedee?" Dreda asked. Her horror of the morning was subsiding.

"The letters V D stand for venereal disease," Abner said. "It's a group of illnesses that spread sexually. Most are treatable, but none of them are things anyone wants to have. It's a practical reason for not having careless sex."

"I'll remember," she promised.

"So if Topsy has sex with a lot of men, she should get pregnant or VD?" Clark asked. He had a natural curiosity about things, especially the supposedly naughty secrets.

"That's it," Abner agreed. "But she doesn't seem to have had any trouble. Either she's quite lucky, or she's more careful than she suggests."

"She's a sopath," Nefer said. "She won't be careful. I'm not."

"You're too young to get pregnant, and have been lucky to avoid VD," Abner said. "Your activity has been more limited. You've had sex with what, ten boys and men? She's had sex with hundreds."

"I guess you're right. She should be knocked up or sick, and she isn't."

"Which may relate to our answer," Bunty said. "If souls are local, then anyone living in a soul-poor area needs to prevent pregnancy, to avoid getting a sopath. They need good contraception."

"That's right," Abner said. "We don't need to control the global population, just bring the birthrate down to the level where souls are available. Especially in areas like this. Contraception can solve the sopath problem."

"Contraception could have solved the population problem long ago," Bunty said. "But too many people are like sopaths in that respect: they simply don't bother. And try to persuade the major religions to preach contraception!"

"Which side are the religions really serving?" Nefer asked. "God or Satan? Not that I care, but I'm curious."

They smiled, knowing it was a joke.

"We're back with that problem," Abner said. "We know how to solve the sopath challenge, but we can't implement it because of religion, carelessness, and ignorance."

"Unless there's a way to have safe sex that those things won't stop," Bunty said. "This is probably a blind alley, but let's ask Autopsy what her secret is."

"She'll say 'Fuck me, Abner, and I'll tell you,'" Nefer said, smiling. "I would."

"Will she settle for holding my hand?"

"She'd rather hold your cock." The others had to smile, appreciating the reference.

"I'll offer my hand," Abner said.

When it was time to sleep, Abner murmured "The watch continues."

They all knew what that meant. He did not trust Autopsy despite her seeming conversion. She was probably faking it. She surely did love Abner, now, but that did not necessarily mean she accepted his family in the way Nefer did. Autopsy was older, and accustomed to having her own way. It was more likely that she would be scheming to eliminate the family so she could have Abner for herself. Because she knew Abner stood by his family, and probably meant the formidable threat he had made on Dreda's behalf, Autopsy was being cautious. She would be looking for a way to get rid of them without implicating herself. Then, by her reckoning, Abner would have no choice but to take what was offered: repeated raw sex with the sopath.

"Do we have to, father?" Nefer asked. "We're safe here, aren't we, under Autopsy's protection?" She was lying, meaning the opposite, as her continuing use of the term indicated.

"It's good discipline," Abner said. "We won't always be in a protected situation. We need to stay in practice."

"We understand, father," Clark said. "It's a pain, but we'll do it."

"A pain, father," Dreda agreed. They were all on board, understanding that they remained in danger.

Nefer took the first watch, walking from room to room in the suite, checking frequently on everyone. Meanwhile Abner and Bunty, pretending assurance of their privacy, made enthusiastic love. Nefer, on her rounds, looked in on them, and nodded; what Autopsy viewed in her film would make her jealous as hell, if she were capable of jealousy.

Then Bunty took her turn on guard, and Nefer lay down beside Abner and took his hand. Again, Autopsy should be jealous, perhaps not of the hand holding specifically, but of Nefer's freedom to lie beside him and touch him as he slept. Nefer was a sopath, and they all knew it, yet she had this privilege. It meant, among other things, that Abner could get friendly with a known sopath, if he trusted her. Autopsy would be pondering that.

The others, including Abner, took their turns. Thus they passed the night in a routine that signified their caution despite their words. That, too, Autopsy would note and ponder.

In the morning they met with Autopsy again, in the dining room for a lavish breakfast. She was conservatively garbed, showing no private flesh, and her hair was bound back into a bun. "I'll tell you right off, I don't use anything when I fuck," she said. "I have no trouble with VD or pregnancy. I'm immune."

"Here is our reasoning," Abner said, not pretending to be surprised. It was a kind of game they were playing, with moves and counter-moves having implications beyond their seeming simplicity. Autopsy was spying on them, and they knew it, and she knew they knew it. "If there's something protective you use, it's very effective. We need to know whether it would work on a global scale."

"There really isn't. Only—" She broke off, pondering.

"There is something," Nefer said.

"It's the grotto." She did not seem to be lying; this was something important to her.

"The what?"

"I go there every day, because it gives me a high. Probably it has no connection, but I can show it to you if you want."

She wanted to show them something. They needed to find out why. Sopaths as a class were not into incidental sightseeing. What was really on her mind? "We had better see it," Abner said.

"Give me your hand. I'll take you there."

There was no further doubt she knew of their evening dia-

logue. She was implying that she would settle for hand holding, as Nefer did. But of course she would not. It had to be a
ploy. "Take us there," Abner said, proffering his hand.

Autopsy took it and led him outside. Her fingers massaged
his fingers as they walked, with a surprisingly erotic effect. "It's
a couple miles away, in the hills. We should drive."

They got into the motor home, and Abner drove while Autopsy sat up front and put her hand on his arm, subtly mas-
saging it too. She really was settling for that, for now, perhaps
considering it an avenue to greater intimacy. He remembered
how she had massaged his penis.

He wondered again why a sopath should desire contact with
any souler. It seemed that even though she lacked a soul, she
missed it, and touching him meant she was also touching his
soul. Sexual intimacy would represent an even closer touch.

"This is nice out in the country," Clark remarked from in
back, evidently looking around. "Will you let us run around
and play, father?" Something the children had no intention of
doing. The family was staying close together.

"If you really want to, son."

They remained on red alert. All of them understood that
there was a vicious animal in their midst that only *looked* like
a lovely young woman. Nefer had educated them well in that
respect.

They parked in the hills below a wooded slope. Autopsy led
him up to a small cave. The grotto was a quiet chamber overgrown with moss. "I don't let anyone else come here," she said.
"It's mine. I think the fruities knew of it, because I've found
some of their trinkets here, but they didn't mess it up. Maybe
they liked the high." She breathed deeply. "Feel it."

They breathed deeply. There was a certain indefinable odor,
not unpleasant, but it did nothing for Abner and evidently not
for Clark. The girls, however—Bunty, Nefer, and Dreda—soon
were truly appreciating it. "There *is* something," Bunty murmured.

Abner looked at her. She was almost glowing, and her

breasts seemed to be pushing against the cloth of her shirt, accentuating her sex appeal. She gazed at him with a certain barely-muted passion that made him want to have sex with her right there where she stood. He had a burgeoning erection that he suspected was partly her appearance and partly her subtle odor reaching his internal triggers.

"You feel it too," Autopsy said wisely.

Abner looked at her, and saw the same sexual passion, un-muted. Then he looked at Nefer, and it was there too. Even little Dreda looked hungry for something. But not Clark, who looked uneasy about the kind of stares the girls were giving him. He could be having a sexual rush that he did not know how to handle. Abner sympathized.

"This is an aphrodisiac environment," Abner said. "That turns on females, who it seems then turn on males with their pheromones or whatever. This explains a little, but not enough."

"The moss," Bunty said. "Maybe there's fungus or lichen, with spores that act like pheromones, turning people. But I'm not sure why, unless it's simply a remarkable coincidence."

"If it is restricted to a special environment, like a cave," Abner said, "it could have trouble propagating. It could send spores out on the wind, but it might be more efficient to use an animal host, the way many plants use bees."

"Flowers don't make bees sexy," Bunty said. "They provide them with sweet food as an inducement. Then their spores or equivalent get carried along when the bees travel."

"But something that made human females like it, might then be able to spread as they interacted with others," Abner said, working it out. "If the spores are delicate, needing a warm moist environment, sex could be a way to transfer them safely."

"How about rabies?" Clark asked, edging toward the cave exit. "That makes animals really mad, and they bite and spread it in their spit."

"Now there's an idea," Abner agreed. "If the spores emulated pheromones and made the host not mad but sexually turned on, that would do it."

"What about no VD?" Nefer asked. Her eyes were wide, her breathing was fast and her mouth wet; she stood with her legs spread as if ready to accommodate intimacy. It was hard to believe she was only seven years old; she seemed to be suffering a genuine sexual arousal.

"A really sharp infection would try to keep a host healthy," Abner said. "So it might fight off other infections, and maybe in the process pregnancy also, since its purpose is to maximize its opportunities to spread. It might want the area of contact, the sex organs, to be reserved for it alone."

"That would explain a lot," Autopsy said. "When I first came here I was six years old and ordinary. But soon I began developing, and I really got interested in sex, and men really got interested in me."

"The fruities!" Nefer said. "They must have found this grotto, and discovered how it made their women sexy without babies. Only they *wanted* babies. So they got the hell out of here to avoid temptation."

"That could certainly explain their abrupt departure," Bunty agreed. "There's no fanatic like a religious fanatic."

Abner glanced again at Bunty, whose measurements seemed to have expanded. He suspected that only her strong interest in fathoming the erotic mystery of the grotto kept her from trying to get him alone for phenomenal passion. "We need to get samples of those spores, or whatever it is in the air here," he said. "It just might be the perfect contraceptive."

"If you want to drop the birth rate," Bunty said, "Give women a contraceptive that not only protects them from VD, but also enhances their sexual desire and allure. They'll use it often, and have no babies, regardless of their religious strictures. Sex appeal is the average woman's real religion, because of the power it can give her over men."

"We may just have our answer," Abner said, excited. "Take samples to a laboratory, isolate the active ingredients, manufacture, package, and distribute them as a turn-on sexiness pill. We wouldn't even have to mention its contraceptive aspect, to avoid religious feedback. People would use it regardless."

"Samples?" Autopsy asked, frowning. This was it seemed not part of her agenda.

"Sections of the moss, the air, the earth, any water here," he explained. "To get them analyzed in a chemical laboratory. To find out how this stuff works. To solve the population problem, and stop the births of more sopaths."

"What's in it for me?"

And of course she didn't care about the possible good for the world. She had her own price.

"Persuade her," Bunty said abruptly. "We'll go search the motor. We should have some jars there for samples." She glanced at the children and Nefer, and the four of them left the cave.

Abner realized that Bunty had had more than enough of the erotic arousal fostered by the grotto and needed to get herself and the girls out of it immediately. It wasn't that she had any objection to sex, but that this artificial promotion of lust was not appropriate to the family setting. She was probably not keen on exposing Clark to the attention of aroused girls, either. Nefer was behaving, but in that environment she might see about seducing the boy, and Clark was surely willing.

Then he remembered her words: "Persuade her." Bunty was not merely extricating herself and the children, she was giving him leave to pay Autopsy's price, so they could get the samples and depart before the day finished. As she had said before, she would put him into bed with an ardent sopath if that was what it took to solve the larger sopath problem once and for all. This just might be that opportunity. Should he take it? Intellectually he realized it might make sense, but emotionally he felt it could be a bad mistake. This was a remorseless sopath!

"Well, now," Autopsy said. "You know what I want, Abner." She opened her blouse.

He was wary, as he had been of her abrupt capitulation the

day before. Yet if they got the samples they could be rapidly done with Sauerkraut. Was it worth it? The potential reward was huge, but he didn't trust her.

She gave him no time to temporize. She threw off her blouse, baring her fine breasts. She wore no bra, being so well formed that she didn't need it. "We have what, maybe five minutes? Time enough. Let's get to it. Take off your pants." She inhaled and exhaled. It was compelling.

Was this conveniently sudden? What was her angle? Yet her sex appeal was phenomenal and his body was responding strongly. It was hard to fight his burgeoning desire. Pheromones were almost certainly turning him on. Still, he tried again. "I really don't think—"

"You don't need to think, Abner." She drew off her skirt. She wore no panties. Yes, she had come prepared, knowing the effect of the grotto, and he distrusted that while being strongly turned on by it.

"If this proves to be the answer we seek, then I will consider having a—a relationship with you. But not right now. We have other things to do."

"Right now or nothing," she said. "Give me what I want, and I'll give you what you want." She stepped close and put her arms around him.

Yes, there had to be pheromones, because her closeness was instantly arousing his passion despite his misgiving. Still he tried to demur, realizing that to yield would be playing into her hands. "There will be time enough later. Right now I want to learn more about this moss."

She drew herself close, lifted on tiptoes, and kissed him. The impact was potent. Suddenly his desire was overwhelming. It was like a dam bursting asunder. He kissed her back, no longer caring that he would probably be safer kissing an anaconda.

Then she was opening his fly to bring out his rampant member. She hauled herself up, then let herself down, and his penis was nudging into her eager cleft. She was thoroughly experienced; she knew how to make the connection no-handed.

In a moment he was plunging into her as they stood, her weight coming down to make the penetration complete and very firm. She kissed him again as he thrust. His ejaculation was immediate, and seemed to last forever, spurting all that he had into her body. There was nothing in the whole world as important as that phenomenal connection.

Yet that was only a portion of it. Autopsy's urgency and joy of the occasion seemed to more than match his own, maybe because she suffered no guilt. It was as if each of his pulses was a wash of sheer bliss for her, enhancing her own continuing orgasm. As if she were drawing passion from him and savoring it like fine wine, which further enhanced his own rapture. Her vagina was rhythmically milking his member, drawing every possible bit of pleasure along with the fluid.

It was the most remarkable sex he had ever had, qualitatively distinguished from routine sex. It was savagely addictive. If regular sex was marijuana, this was cocaine.

She had him. All he wanted was her favor, in the hope of further fulfillment like this. She had mentioned how she controlled the souler men of Kraut by dispensing her favor sparingly and giving sex once a week per man, if he behaved. That had seemed inadequate to control grown men. Abner understood now that it wasn't. She had imprinted on him a new desire that could never be completely satisfied. He wanted the ambiance of her nearness, the pleasure of doing her bidding, the delight of her passing favor. The rapture of her pheromones. Exactly as her other men did.

His copious ejaculation dribbled to its conclusion and his member started softening, but the pleasure of contact with her remained. It wasn't limited to sex. His phenomenal orgasm had been magnified because it was *for her*, giving her pleasure. It was becoming a memory, but his delight in touching her remained. He was utterly besotted with her. She had turned the tables on him, fascinating him the way he had hoped to fascinate her. He had become her love slave.

She slid off his member and dropped to the floor. "Now you are mine," she said, satisfied as she found a cloth in a cubbyhole and mopped the semen welling from her cleft. "You may still try to fight it, but the hook is in, and you will inevitably succumb."

Abner did not answer, because he could not refute it. She had conquered him, and knew it. His penis was spent, and was going limp, but already he was thinking of the next time he might have her. Whatever she wanted of him he would do, for the promise of that next fulfillment. She was simply the most remarkable female creature he could imagine.

This was the trap she had made for him. To bring him here, isolate him, and overwhelm him sexually. Simple, straightforward, and infernally effective. He had walked right into it. Had her nearness, her hand holding, quietly compelled him so that he had not really resisted? She had made him react the day before, tempting him, setting him up for this more serious effort. And Bunty, thinking that one indulgence would satisfy him, had let him do it. She had miscalculated too, underestimating the thoroughness of the desire. Autopsy was not the child Nefer; she was a fully developed and competent woman, buttressed by the pheromones.

"You will not be traveling again," Autopsy said as she completed her cleanup. "You will remain here, and service me often, because with you it's not a duty but a pleasure. I simply had to capture you, because you're the most man I have encountered. It will take me some time to tire of you." As a sopath she had no inclination to relate to his feelings; she had taken him prisoner and now was establishing the routine.

"I have a family," he said weakly.

She shrugged. "We'll find a use for it, I'm sure. Except for the sopath. She put a knife to my throat; she must die."

And he dared not argue, because Bunty was surely next on Autopsy's list of nuisances. He still loved Bunty, but would not be able to protect her from Autopsy's wrath. He had to do his utmost to ensure that wrath was never aroused. If that meant servicing her frequently, as she put it, well, he was eager to do exactly that.

Autopsy nodded, not yet dressing. She was letting him gaze at her perfect body, cementing his desire for it. He knew that if he pleased her, he would see that body often, and sometimes touch it. "I see you understand. Behave, and I will treat you well."

Behave. Do her bidding without question. Then she would reward him with her favor, and sometimes with sex. She was his mistress in both senses of the word. He felt his penis thickening again. Yet at the same time he hated the trap he had fallen into. He was bound and gagged, his personal will overridden by hers. He had to break out, yet knew he could not.

There was the sound of an explosion outside. They both hurried to the cave opening and looked out.

There below was the blasted motor home, with an ugly roiling cloud of smoke rising from it. "Bunty!" Abner cried in horror.

"Something must have happened," Autopsy said, unperturbed. "Maybe someone thought I was in there, and tried to take me out. Too bad for your family."

Abner stared at her. "You arranged this! You set it up. You got me alone in the grotto, distracted by sex, while they went down to the vehicle you knew your minions had booby-trapped!"

She shrugged. "And what if I did? They were impediments anyway. It was the sopath I was after. If the others went in with her, well, they were collateral damage. Now I have you all to myself, without complications."

Abner had been overwhelmed by sex. Now a different emotion surfaced: the shock of grief translating rapidly to outrage. "I said I'd kill you if you harmed my family."

She smiled, facing him with her ideal naked body almost glowing. "Oh? Maybe you did. What are you going to do, Abner, with no hot poker handy? Fuck me to death?" She glanced at his penis, which was stirring.

She had conquered him, but had overplayed her hand. Now his sick fury overrode his desire. "I'll rape you with cold steel." He drew his knife.

She laughed. "Do it. I'm calling your bluff, and will punish you for it later." She dropped to the mossy floor and spread her legs wide. "Here's the place, Abner. Put it in there!" She held her labia apart, exactly as Nefer had when they first interacted, only in this case it supercharged his returning desire. He was desperate to get into that aperture, to pump out whatever fluid remained in him, filling her up again. She was flaunting her power over him, daring him to make good on a threat she thought had become impossible for him to honor. Rubbing his face in his helplessness. Punishing him for even trying to escape her control. He knew that this was just the beginning; she would make him violate all his ethical and moral principles, just because she could. He would have to torture others on her say-so, as her other minions did.

He had to follow through.

Abner dropped to the ground beside her, put a knee on her chest to hold her down, positioned the blade, and rammed it into the slit. The motion was sexual in its fashion, a sadistic turn-on as he saw the steel disappear into her.

Autopsy screamed, as much in surprise as in pain. He had indeed raped her with the knife.

She struggled, her breasts pushing against his knee, but he held her down. She could match neither his strength nor his ferocity, and the thrust had severely wounded her.

He drew the knife out, and thrust it in again, deeper, like a deadly phallus. He stabbed her repeatedly in the groin, twisting the blade as he did so. Hot blood spurted out like a red ejaculation, covering the knife and his hand, pooling on the ground. He kept on stabbing and cutting as her belly was minced from inside.

Suddenly she quieted. "Now you have nothing," she gasped, and died.

Abner's blind rage abated. He had murdered her, and now

he had nothing. He realized that part of his motivation had been to get free of her, and that her death was the only way. He'd had to do it immediately, because he would never have been able to summon the will later. He would have been her love-slave, like the other men of the town. He had his promised vengeance, and nothing else. She was right about that one thing.

He got up and staggered out of the grotto. What was he to do? Everything he valued had been lost. Again. Only this time it was worse than before. He had loved his prior family, but he had come to love his second family more. Now, in the agony of his loss, he could see that.

"Daddy!"

It was Dreda, running toward the cave, disheveled and frightened. She had survived!

He bent to scoop her up into his embrace. "I thought you were dead!" he said.

"Nefer saved us," she said, clinging tearfully to him. "We're all alive."

Abner was stunned by relief. He sank to the ground, sobbing. Dreda hugged him, trying to comfort him. It really did help.

It seemed only a moment before the others were with them. Then he learned what had happened.

The four of them had entered the motor home, searching for jars. Then Nefer had spoken up. "I smell a bomb, like the one Abner and I set off."

"A bomb?" Bunty asked, not focusing.

"And I hear it ticking! It'll blow in maybe half a minute. GET OUT OF HERE!"

They piled out and ran from the vehicle. Perhaps ten seconds later the bomb went off. The blast was like a huge hand smacking their backsides, but they were far enough away to escape damage. Then, fearful of some other attack, they had hidden in the brush.

The bomb had evidently been set to be primed when the

door opened, to detonate perhaps a minute later, so that they all had time to get inside. Autopsy had to have ordered it, knowing that Bunty would not care to remain long in the grotto. It had been a good plan, and it had almost worked.

So Nefer had saved them all. Abner owed her again. Yet she was a sopath, like Autopsy only younger. "How am I ever going to repay you?" he asked her.

She smiled, knowing he knew her price. "I'll think of something, Abner. I got a jar; I'll get the sample."

"It's ugly in there." But she was already on her way.

"Ugly?" Bunty asked.

Now Abner realized that there was blood on his arm and shirt, and some had spread to Dreda. "When I thought you were all dead, I knifed her," he said grimly. "She had—had ensorcelled me, with her hormones, but she misjudged my reaction to her treachery."

"Ensorcelled?" Bunty asked.

"She seduced me. I tried to fight it, and could not. I'm sorry."

"Don't be. I know how it was in there. Even Clark had an erection from those spreading hormones. I told you to do it. I thought it was a fair exchange for the possible solution to the entire sopath problem." She smiled. "I also thought it was your chance to possess an outstanding body, one time. I thought you'd like that."

She was certainly not the jealous type. But she too had miscalculated. "She was trying to capture me and kill the rest of you. That was no fair exchange. Ah, Bunty, if I lost you--"

She kissed him. "I understand. I really do. You love me and I love you. If she had killed you, I'd have butchered her in an instant."

"Oh Bunty, I love you so much!" They kissed again, Dreda between them. Neither Clark nor Dreda protested. They would not have protested if Abner and Bunty had sex right there. It was one of the elements that held their oddly formed family together. Probably they were still being affected by the ambiance of the grotto, the stimulated hormones. It didn't matter; their love was real regardless.

Nefer returned with the closed jar, unfazed by what she had seen. "Did you fuck her first?"

"I fucked her," Abner agreed. "Then I slew her."

"She did not know you as well as I do. I'd have been more careful. I'd have known not to try to hurt your family."

Nefer was a child. But she would not remain one long. The time was apt to come when she, aided by the pheromones, had the body and desire of Autopsy. But that was a future problem. "See that you never forget," Abner told her.

"Someone there," Nefer said alertly, gazing down at the bombed motor home. "Someone making sure we're dead, maybe."

"We need to get out of here before they discover the body," Bunty said, alarmed.

"Abner can call in another mortar strike," Nefer said. "Zero in on our position, then move on so the pursuers are there when it lands. Then we can call Pariah and have them send a van to pick us up and spirit us away."

"You're quite the organizer," Bunty said.

"It comes with the territory of being a genius. I want to save my own hide."

"What do you think, dear?" Bunty asked Abner. She was always careful to defer to him with major decisions, in private and in public, promoting his authority. He rather liked that.

"I think there's no need for heroics," Abner said. "It should be easy to take over this town. I doubt Autopsy had the wit to establish any formal government other than her whim, or any second in command. With her gone, it will be chaos until a new sopath takes her place. That would be a waste of a perfect opportunity."

"I don't follow."

"We are going to need a manufacturing plant to make the fungus pheromone product."

"Fungo," Clark said.

Abner laughed, and that was a relief. The horror of Autopsy was already fading. Then he reconsidered. "Fungo as in fun, and as in fungus," he said. "I believe you have named it, Clark."

"Yeah," Clark said, pleased.

"Anyway," Abner continued, "If we want to circulate this contraceptive globally, why give it away to a big soulless company that will seek to maximize profits rather than distribution? We can start out by distributing it free, then charge a modest amount as it catches on. Soon enough the demand will become huge. We'll need more than a garage laboratory to refine it. We will have here a complete town in need of employment, and this can provide it. Souler adults to handle the various aspects competently, sopath children to test samples."

"But it's an aphrodisiac!" Bunty protested.

"Those girls have been whoring in Sweetpea all along. This will not only enhance their business, it will keep them sterile and VD free. It will give them options to advance themselves in ways other than sexual. That's an improvement."

"I suppose it is," she agreed thoughtfully.

"It promotes orgasm in the woman, too," he said. "I saw it and felt it in Autopsy. She was climaxing as powerfully as I was. Sexual equality in the truest sense."

"We shall have to verify that soon," she said. "That alone would make it commercially irresistible."

"This can be our base for saving the world," he said grandly. "All we need to do is organize it."

"What's in it for me?" Nefer asked, echoing Autopsy's question.

And there was the problem. They did owe her, but she was a sopath. "What do you want?"

"Your favor. To be part of your family. To start."

It was that "to start" that made him especially cautious. "You want Bunty and me to adopt you into the family, as we did Clark and Dreda?"

"She did save us," Dreda said.

"You're not my sister!" Clark protested with surprising vehemence.

"I'll never be your sister," Nefer agreed, eying him. She returned to Abner. "But I do want to be Nefer Slate when I mature."

That was what he had feared. She had a larger design, and they could not ignore it. "I'm not going to marry you, regardless how you mature," Abner said. "I am more than satisfied with Bunty, and yes, I am prepared to kill anyone who tries to kill her. You know that. One experience with Autopsy was far more than enough." He realized that now that Autopsy was dead, he no longer cared about her. She had compelled him with fascination and transcendent sex, not true love.

"I was thinking maybe of being a second wife."

A larger design indeed!

"Not in this culture," Bunty said. "One wife at a time is the limit. But if you mean to be his mistress, when you're grown, there are problems there too."

Abner was glad to have her take over this dialogue. She had a perspective he lacked.

"What problems?" Nefer asked.

"A mistress does not take her lover's name."

"Oh." That evidently set the girl back. "What else?"

"By the time you are grown, your crush on Abner will have faded. You will be more interested in boys your own age. So he can't promise you anything now that will survive the passage of time. It would be a deceit, and therefore cheat you of a reward you surely deserve."

Nefer's jaw dropped. "I'll be damned!"

"You think about it," Bunty said. "We will do right by you. You just need to come to better understand your true will."

Bunty just might have saved him some extreme future awkwardness. When Nefer matured physically, enhanced by the pheromones, she would be as compelling as Autopsy had been. "Did I mention that I love you?" he asked her.

"Not often enough. Now let's attend to that man." For the

man they had seen was walking purposefully toward them.

"I'll take it from here," Abner said. He raised a hand, hailing the man. "You're one of Autopsy's minions."

The man nodded. "Yes."

"She had you plant a bomb in our motor home."

"Yes. I do what she tells me to."

"Well, things have changed. My family escaped the bomb, but it annoyed me, and I stabbed Autopsy to death. You will now take your orders from me."

That brought the man up short. "You killed her?"

"Go into the grotto and see the body. Then convey us to your vehicle. We're going into town, where I will address the citizens. There will be a new order, and chances are your lives will markedly improve. Get moving."

The man hesitated, then walked on past them toward the grotto.

"A new order," Nefer repeated. "I think I'm going to like this."

"You should," Abner said. "You will be one of my chief lieutenants, helping me get important things done."

"Gee," she said, pleased. "And can I hold your hand?"

"Often," he agreed. He saw that Bunty, Clark, and Dreda approved. He had found a way to keep Nefer satisfied without displacing any of them.

They all had a phenomenal future to explore.

AFTERWORD

That was the turning point. The samples proved workable, and a formula developed for the "cosmetic" supplement Fungo. The spores were imperfectly adapted to the human species, and unable to convert a woman's body into a spore-making machine. Thus the effect was limited to a few hours before it faded, but they were phenomenal hours. Soon after application it rendered an average adult woman into a fervent beauty emitting pheromones that could rapidly seduce almost any man. Her newfound desire for sex made her ardent, and she climaxed as rapidly as her partner did. Each use caused her body to shape up further, in that respect being cumulative. It was addictive in the sense that she craved additional sexual fulfillment, but when she stopped using it, that craving subsided and she returned to normal without withdrawal pangs.

The fact that none of these women could conceive was not advertised, though before long religious groups struggled without much success to suppress Fungo. Samples were at first distributed free, then more was made available at a moderate price. The demand ballooned, and the facility at the town of Sauerkraut had to strain to keep up. Licenses were granted, and the phenomenon became global. All over the world the birth rate dropped dramatically. Most women simply were not interested in giving up their hourglass figures and enhanced sex appeal for the sake of having more babies, and the men they associated with were glad to support their decision. It is generally agreed that there is no sex like Fungo sex.

With the descent of the birth rate, the problem of the sopaths faded and before long was almost forgotten. Few cared to remember how difficult it had been. Some folk even claimed that there never had been a sopath problem; that it was an urban legend circulated to terrify young married couples.

Today the global population is only half what it was, and still declining. Those who choose to have children are assured that they will have souls. Many women cease taking Fungo at the time they wish to conceive, then resume using it once they birth their babies. The point is that today there are virtually no unwanted babies. There is an enormous amount of sex, but hardly any venereal disease. It is a better world, thanks to Abner Slate, who is now retired with his wife Bunty. His children remain active in the Fungo project at Sauerkraut, regarding it as highly beneficial to mankind despite the condemnation of many religious groups. Dreda Slate now runs the operation, traveling widely to demonstrate its effect, and has been described as the world's sexiest CEO.

One of the most important achievements of Abner Slate's effort was his demonstration that it was after all possible to tame and civilize sopaths by providing them with sufficient motive and stern discipline. They did not have to be killed. He proved this by allowing one of them to associate closely with his own family, even with his children. Some might liken it to having a pet crocodile uncaged in the house: you have to exercise constant caution, but such pets do have their satisfactions.

I wish to thank all those who facilitated my research for this volume, especially my father Abner, my mother Bunty, and my sister Dreda. Especially my smart, lovely, and passionate wife, the soul singer Nefer Slate, whose eidetic memory and merciless objectivity greatly improved the detail.

Clark Slate

AUTHOR'S NOTE

I have been trying to tie up loose ends as I get older, so as not to leave any projects unfinished. I am 75 at this writing, and while there is as yet no clear indication of my termination, chances are it will occur in the next decade or three. *The Sopaths* is the last one of any magnitude. Another reason I scheduled it for this time is that the death of my elder daughter from cancer—melanoma—in 2009 put me in the depressed mood for horror, which is not normally to my taste. That seems to have been effective.

The project dates way back. My earliest penciled note is dated 9-11-80: "Notion: when the souls run out. World population burgeons so much that the supply of new souls is exhausted, and so babies start being born without souls. This could be a horror story." The underlying assumption being that the soul is the source of empathy, conscience, remorse, and emotional appreciation for the arts, which I see as deriving from empathy. In science, these things may derive from mirror neurons, which echo our feelings as events happen, enabling us to relive the associated feelings and to relate them to others, feeling their feelings. Empathy may be the foundation of what makes us human. Perhaps, for this novel, we could assume that it is the soul that activates the mirror neurons.

I started collecting newspaper clippings relating to man's inhumanity to man, to serve as inspiration and relevance, and the earliest ones date from that time on. In the course of a decade there were so many I just had to stop. Here's a random sample: in 1979 a Milwaukee waitress and her boyfriend picked up a pair of hitchhikers, who then killed him and beat and raped her and left her for dead. Her skull was fractured with a tire iron, but she survived and identified them. At the trial they showed no emotion, being blank and staring. They smirked and giggled to themselves, as if it were a big joke. The legal maneuvers dragged on for years, with the brothers constantly escaping and being caught, showing no remorse. They were essentially sopaths, creatures without conscience. That was just one of hundreds of similarly sickening items.

I made more pencil notes in 1981, the project now titled *Angst*. Somewhere in the world a woman owed two men money, so she denounced them as guerrillas, and the police killed them. There were two more men at the bus stop, so the woman denounced them too, and the police killed them. All the men were innocent. I saw how that could apply to my story: denounce people as sopaths and get them killed. There were items of mass starvation in Africa, where resources went instead to making further war. That could be considered a sopath government. There was a TV program on mercenary soldiers: ideal employment for sopaths who don't care whom they hurt as long as they get theirs. Penciled note in 1985 about prison rape and public indifference to it. Sopaths in and out of prison, no? I made a note: "A girl could attack a man sexually, and blame him for attacking her. Sopaths can cause innocent people to be condemned by others."

In 1986 I retitled the project *The Sopaths*, but it remained too ugly to write. The news items continued. In 1991 was one about a twelve-year-old boy raping a four-year-old girl. There was reference to eight- and nine-year-old boys sexually abusing a nine-year-old girl at a playground. I realized that sexual abuse isn't limited to adults. Also that the sopath problem would manifest long before the soulless children reached adulthood, and would have to be dealt with then. So most of my huge collection of horrors became irrelevant. My last clippings are dated 1998; that aspect seemed pointless to continue.

Still I did not write the novel. It was simply too horrible for my taste. The project languished.

Finally I realized that I didn't *have* to have the story as ugly as the clippings showed. I could lighten up on the detail and address the underlying problem: overpopulation and the exhaustion of the supply of souls. In fact, at times during the writing I discovered that it wasn't horrible enough, as I moved the ugliness off-stage, and I had to restore some of it to maintain a proper balance.

That made it viable, and on February 7, 2001 I typed formal notes for the story. It was to be in three stages: first the babies born without souls and the horror one family experiences, and the reconstitution of a family of survivors. Second realization by society of the sopath menace and the need to kill sopaths. Third, the horror of the discovery that it didn't matter if some souled people were killed, because their souls would be returned to the pool and be reborn. Thus there could be wholesale slaughter, in the name of saving the world. Still plenty ugly.

I used it as a trial project to test the word processor Word Perfect in the Linux operating system, which I was then switching to. I wrote the first chapter, but the word processor was difficult and balky. My note for February 14, 2001 says, "Word-Perfect locked up, costing me my last 60 words of notes, but not any text, I think." By the end of the month I was satisfied that I did not want that word processor, and that repulsion spread to the novel I had been using it on, and I set it aside.

In February 2010 I returned to it, this time trying out the Ubuntu Linux distribution with a word processor I liked and had been using for years, OpenOffice. Heavy reading piled in—I don't read so much for pleasure as for business—soaking up my working time, and then my wife tripped, fell, and fractured her left elbow and right knee. She was in the emergency room, in the hospital, then at a rehabilitation center, and it was most of a month before I got her back. When she returned she was still in recovery, restricted to the house, using wheelchair and walker. I ran the house, making meals, doing laundry, shopping and so on, and managed to keep it on an even keel, but my working time was only a fraction what it had been. Thus it took four months to write the 65,000 word novel, when in prior times

I had written 60,000 words a month. Fortunately I had no other projects at that time, and could take the time I needed. I am well into retirement age, but I will never retire alive. I will always be writing something, and speed is not of the essence. My next project will be another funny fantasy Xanth novel, a considerable contrast to *The Sopaths*.

I have written more than 140 books in my career so far, and each has its separate cast of characters. I try to avoid repeating names, but having used thousands, I find it an increasing challenge to come up with new ones. I have books of first names, and turn the pages looking for ones I haven't used before. I don't think I have used Abner before; it reminds me of the famous comic strip Li'l Abner. Similarly Clark; I have known people with that name but never used it. Similarly Dreda, once common, now out of fashion, the name reminding me of the spinning toy dreidel. And Bunty. When I was a baby my parents were doing relief work in Spain during the Spanish Civil War of 1937-40 and left my sister and me with our maternal grandparents in England, who hired a nanny, who I believe was a teenaged Scottish girl named Bunty. It was I think only for a couple of years, but my earliest memories are of being cared for by Bunty, who seemed like my mother. In fact I was severely disappointed when my real mother took us back and we traveled to Spain and then to America, barely escaping World War Two in Europe. That emotional disruption may account for my later emergence as a fiction writer; that sort of thing is typical of the breed, who it seems need to be jolted out of their comfortable tracks and thrown into limbo for a period to evoke their imaginative creativity. It was not a pleasant experience, and for a time I felt I would have been better off never to have existed. I never saw Bunty again, and don't know what became of her, but the experience remains as my memory of happiness before the darkness claimed me. That name seemed fitting for the role in this novel, a woman who became an effective mother to two unrelated children in need.

This was conceived as a horror novel, and it is that, but I

found that it has also an environmental and perhaps a theological theme of a sort. In this case it's not the viability of air, earth, and sea that mankind's overpopulation is despoiling, but the supply of souls. I am agnostic and have no belief in the supernatural, and I regard souls as fantasy. But I should think those who do believe should have a care not to exhaust this resource too. So far they don't seem to care, though the world is horribly hostage to the consequence. As Nefer asks in the novel: is religion really serving God or Satan? I think that's a damn good question. If the intention is to serve God and preserve and protect the world God gave us, this business about procreation at any price has to go. Since sex can't be abolished, or people's desire for it—after all, God made these things too—there needs to be effective contraception. If not—then maybe we do know which side is being served.

I suspect this may be a traditionally unpublishable novel, not because of its occasional gore or the horror of its thesis, but because it recognizes the sexuality of children, which would be unleashed by those without conscience, as they are in real life. The horror and erotic markets are girt about by as many taboos as are other genres, and certain aspects of reality are avoided. So be it. I showed the sopaths the way I believe they really would be. Though I write fantasy, without believing in it, I do believe that the concept of souls being the key to conscience and human empathy is a useful way to address the problem that mankind's unfettered exploitation of the planet is causing. We need to clean up our act soon, or we will all suffer a horrendous crash. Desperation and hunger will make people become indistinguishable from sopaths, their mischief magnified because they won't be children.

Hereafter, the serious material covered, I will return to writing light fantasy. I enjoy that, and it is easy to do, as this present novel was not.

—Piers Anthony, June 10, 2010.

PIERS ANTHONY:
AN AUTOBIOGRAPHICAL SKETCH

I was born in Oxford, England, in AwGhost, 1934. My parents both graduated from the university at Oxford, but I was slow from the outset. I spent time with relatives and a nanny while my parents went to do relief work in Spain during the Spanish Civil War of 1936-39. They were helping to feed the children rendered hungry by the devastation of the war. When that ended, my sister and I joined them in Spain. I left my native country at the age of four—and never returned. The new government of General Franco in Spain, evidently error-prone and suspicious of foreigners doing good works, arrested my father in 1940. They refused to admit that they had done so, making him in effect a "disappeared" person, but he was able to smuggle out a note. Then rather than admit error, they let him out on condition that he leave the country. World War II was then in progress, so instead of returning to England, we went to my father's country. In this manner I came to America at age six, on what I believe was the last ship out. Though I was too young to understand what was going on, in time I learned, and I retain an abiding hostility to dictatorships.

My parents' marriage grew strained and finally foundered. Suffering the consequences of separation from my first country and my second country as well as the stress of a family going wrong, I showed an assortment of complications such as nervous tics of head and hands, bed-wetting, and inability to learn. It required three years and five schools to get me through first grade. I later gained intellectual ground, but lost physical ground. When I entered my ninth school in ninth grade I was at the proper level but not the proper size, being the smallest person, male or female, in my class. However, boarding school, and later college, became a better home for me than what I had, and I managed to grow almost another foot by the time I got my BA in writing at Goddard College, Vermont, in 1956. This was just as well, because I married a tall girl I met in college; I had to grow, literally, to meet the challenge.

When I was discharged from the Army in 1959, my wife and I decided to move to Florida. We had family there, and the winters were warm. I had spent several years going to school in the cold winters in Vermont and I do not like the cold weather. I do like the mountainous scenery so we live in north-central Florida where it is hilly, rather than flat.

I had the hodgepodge of employments typical of writers. Of about fifteen types of work I tried, ranging from aide at a mental hospital to technical writer at an electronics company, only one truly appealed: the least successful. But the dream remained. Finally in 1962 my wife agreed to go to work for a year, so that I could stay home and try to write fiction full time. The agreement was that if I did not manage to sell anything, I would give up the dream and focus on supporting my family. As it happened, I sold two stories, earning $160. But such success seemed inadequate to earn a living. So I became an English teacher, didn't like that either, and in 1966 retired again to writing. This time I wrote novels instead of stories, and with them I was able to earn a living. As with the rest of my life, progress was slow, but a decade later I got into light fantasy with the first of my ongoing Xanth series of novels, A Spell for Chameleon, and that proved to be the golden ring. And I wrote two other fantasy series: the Adept novels and the Incarnations of Immortality. My sales and income soared, and I became one of the most successful writers of the genre, with twenty-one NEW YORK TIMES paperback bestsellers in the space of a decade. This enabled us to send our two daughters to college, and drove the wolf quite far from our door. We now live on a tree farm, and would love to have a wolf by our door, but do have deer and wild cat and other wildlife. I am an environmentalist.

But a writer does not live by frivolous fantasy alone. I turned back to serious writing with direct comment on sexual abuse in Firefly, and on history in novels like Tatham Mound, which relates to the fate of the American Indians, and the Geodyssey series, covering man's past three and a half million years to the present, and Volk (available via the Internet), which shows love and death in Civil War Spain and World War II Germany. So I close the circle, returning in my writing to the realm I left as a child. And I have a new, less frivolous fantasy series, ChroMagic, that begins with Key to Havoc. There has always been a serious side to my writing, even in my fantasy, and my readers respond to it. They tell me that I have taught many to read, by showing them that reading could be fun, and that I have saved the lives of some, by addressing concerns such as suicide. I take my readers as seriously as I take my writing, a number of them have become collaborators in a series of joint novels. My autobiography to age 50, Bio of an Ogre, is now out-of-print; there is a sequel, How Precious Was That While. I have had 140 books published, with more in the pipeline.

In fact I am a workaholic, and I love my profession. I have, of course, an ongoing battle with critics, who see only the frivolous level; it is doubtful whether my work will ever in my lifetime receive much critical applause, but I believe in its validity for the longer haul. So do my readers.

ABOUT THE COVER ARTIST

Dan Henk is a professional tattoo artist and illustrator living in Austin, Texas. He does a regular comic for Tattoo Artist Magazine and illustrations for TTA Press. He recently completed his first novel, *By Demons Driven*.

Visit him online at www.danhenk.com.

CPSIA information can be obtained at www.ICGtesting.com
Printed in the USA
BVOW020034240412

288437BV00001BA/4/P